Praise fo

"A luminous and ve

—El.......................
of Rebel Girls and coauthor of the
New York Times bestselling *Good Night
Stories for Rebel Girls: 100 Tales of
Extraordinary Women*

"*The Caravaggio Syndrome* is a daring and often delicious feat
of imagination, as mercurial and masterful as the painter
himself, and filled with surprises at every turn. Alessandro
Giardino has written a genre-expanding novel sure to please
artists, philosophers, Italophiles, and anyone who simply
loves a good story."

—Christopher Castellani, *Los Angeles Times*
and *New York Times* bestselling
author of *Leading Men: A Novel*

"*The Caravaggio Syndrome* is the dramatic convergence of
five characters in two different centuries, beautifully woven
together. It's a book about love, resistance, escape, and
solitude."

—Dalal Mawad, CNN Senior Producer,
award-winning journalist, and author of
*All She Lost: The Explosion in Lebanon,
the Collapse of a Nation and the
Women Who Survive*

"In a genre-bending triptych that is both expansive and
intimate, Alessandro Giardino paints a vibrant *tableau
vivant* that is a bold yet graceful study of life, love, and art.
Smart and sexy, the ambitious work is vividly imaginative

and ornate, offering the reader a literary tour of Naples, Paris, and New York, and reminding us about the important lessons we can learn when we look to the past. A talent to watch!"

—Christopher DiRaddo, author of
The Geography of Pluto: A Novel

"While looking to the past, Alessandro Giardino's inventive mash-up of art history and speculative fiction has a lot to say about our present moment."

—Pedro Ponce, author of *The Devil
and the Dairy Princess: Stories*

"In this surprising debut novel, Alessandro Giardino's writing moves on the page like the wing of a Baroque angel. It doubles and unfolds revealing the Caravaggesque play of light and shadow that unites the lives of its protagonists."

—Gian Maria Annovi, professor of Italian at
the University of Southern California
and author of *Pier Paolo Pasolini:
Performing Authorship*

"This novel enchants, seduces, and transports Naples into the echo of different eras, all coming together through the voice of the author as in a play of mirrors where Caravaggio's appearance is nothing more than another hiding strategy."

—Mariella Pandolfi, professor emerita
of anthropology at Université
de Montréal, Canada

"Alessandro Giardino's debut novel is an incredible achievement and an exciting read: it takes us on a journey between North America and Europe, between the 2000s and the late sixteenth century, through genders, cultures, and artistic genres, alternating intellectual musings and sensual impulses. The complexity of this concise tale is carried and enhanced by incredibly rich language, as timeless as it is poignant."

—Itay Sapir, professor of art history
at Université du Québec à
Montréal, Canada

The Caravaggio Syndrome

Titles in the **Other Voices of Italy** series:

Carmine Abate, *The Round Dance*. Translated by Michelangelo La Luna

Giuseppe Berto, *Glory: The Gospel of Judas, A Novel*. Translated by Gregory Conti

Giuseppe Berto, *Oh, Serafina! A Fable of Love, Lunacy, and Ecology*. Translated by Gregory Conti

Adrián N. Bravi, *My Language Is a Jealous Lover*. Translated by Victoria Offredi Poletto and Giovanna Bellesia Contuzzi

Angelo Cannavacciuolo, *When Things Happen*. Translated by Gregory Pell

Shirin Ramzanali Fazel, *Islam and Me: Narrating a Diaspora*. Translated by Shirin Ramzanali Fazel and Simone Brioni

Alessandro Giardino, *The Caravaggio Syndrome*. Translated by Joyce Myerson and Alessandro Giardino

Geneviève Makaping, *Reversing the Gaze: What If the Other Were You?* Translated by Giovanna Bellesia Contuzzi and Victoria Offredi Poletto

Dacia Maraini, *In Praise of Disobedience: Clare of Assisi*. Translated by Jane Tylus

Dacia Maraini, *Life, Brazen and Garish: A Tale of Three Women*. Translated by Elvira Di Fabio

Porpora Marcasciano, *AntoloGaia: Queering the Seventies, A Radical Trans Memoir*. Translated by Francesco Pascuzzi and Sandra Waters

Luigi Pirandello, *The Outcast*. Translated by Bradford A. Masoni

OVOI

Other Voices of Italy

Series Editors: Alessandro Vettori, Sandra Waters, and Eilis Kierans

This series presents texts in a variety of genres originally written in Italian. Much like the symbiotic relationship between the wolf and the raven, its principal aim is to introduce new or past authors—who have until now been marginalized—to an English-speaking readership. This series also highlights contemporary transnational authors, as well as writers who have never been translated or who are in need of a fresh/contemporary translation. The series further aims to increase the appreciation of translation as an art form that enhances the importance of cultural diversity.

Intertwining the vast topics of Italian Renaissance art history, trauma, and queer relationships, the current book finds itself at home in this book series. The purpose of this novel is to provide historical, mystical, and visual depth to Italian queer fiction set in rural academia as well as the grand metropolises of Naples, Paris, and New York. Leyla is an independent and strong-willed woman whose career is put at risk by an unplanned pregnancy and the re-emergence of childhood traumas connected to the Italian-Turkish branch of her family. Michael, timid and solitary in appearance, possesses a spirit of independence and the appeal of a young man who has grown up in haphazard fashion like a wild and untamed creature. Engaged by Leyla as a research assistant, Michael has a second and less noble reason for cultivating this professional relationship with her: he is in fact infatuated with

Pablo, her simple but inept companion—and father to her child—towards whom he feels an immediate and passionate connection, as well as an inexplicable maternal instinct. What ultimately unites Leyla and Michael is much more than an inconveniently shared romantic partner or common cultural interests. Caravaggio's painting *The Seven Works of Mercy,* secretly inspired by the heretical teachings of Tommaso Campanella, serves as a resonating chamber for the experiences of abuse and mourning endured by Michael and Leyla—but also the gateway to a new and more fulfilling life.

The Caravaggio Syndrome

~

A Novel

ALESSANDRO GIARDINO

Translated by Joyce Myerson
and Alessandro Giardino

Foreword by Ara H. Merjian

Rutgers University Press
New Brunswick, Camden, and Newark, New Jersey
London and Oxford

Rutgers University Press is a department of Rutgers, The State University of New Jersey, one of the leading public research universities in the nation. By publishing worldwide, it furthers the University's mission of dedication to excellence in teaching, scholarship, research, and clinical care.

Library of Congress Cataloging-in-Publication Data
Names: Giardino, Alessandro, author. | Myerson, Joyce, translator. | Merjian, Ara H., 1974- writer of foreword.
Title: The Caravaggio syndrome: a novel / Alessandro Giardino; translated by Joyce Myerson and Alessandro Giardino; foreword by Ara H. Merjian.
Other titles: Sindrome di Caravaggio. English
Description: New Brunswick: Rutgers University Press, 2024. | Series: Other voices of Italy
Identifiers: LCCN 2023026602 | ISBN 9781978839496 (paperback) | ISBN 9781978839502 (hardcover) | ISBN 9781978839519 (epub) | ISBN 9781978839526 (pdf)
Subjects: LCGFT: Novels.
Classification: LCC PQ4907.I29 C3713 2024 | DDC 853/.92—dc23/eng/20230609
LC record available at https://lccn.loc.gov/2023026602

A British Cataloging-in-Publication record for this book is available from the British Library.

Translation copyright © 2024 by Alessandro Giardino and Joyce Myerson
Foreword copyright © 2024 by Ara H. Merjian

Translation of *Sindrome di Caravaggio*. Edizioni Magmata, 2021
No part of this book may be reproduced or utilized in any form or by any means, electronic or mechanical, or by any information storage and retrieval system, without written permission from the publisher. Please contact Rutgers University Press, 106 Somerset Street, New Brunswick, NJ 08901. The only exception to this prohibition is "fair use" as defined by U.S. copyright law. References to internet websites (URLs) were accurate at the time of writing. Neither the author nor Rutgers University Press is responsible for URLs that may have expired or changed since the manuscript was prepared.

∞ The paper used in this publication meets the requirements of the American National Standard for Information Sciences—Permanence of Paper for Printed Library Materials, ANSI Z39.48-1992.

rutgersuniversitypress.org

And so, I became aware of the seemingly paradoxical fact that precisely some of the grandest and most overwhelming creations of art remain obscure to our understanding.
—Sigmund Freud, *The Moses of Michelangelo*

What then? I am Medea and I let them live?
—Luigi Cherubini, *Médée*

Contents

List of Illustrations   xi

Foreword: Caravaggio, Convergences,
Craquelure   xiii
ARA H. MERJIAN

Translator's Note   xvii
JOYCE MYERSON

Author's Note   xix
ALESSANDRO GIARDINO

Preface   xxiii

Prologue: Tommaso Campanella   1

Part 1

1. Leyla   7

2. Tommaso Campanella   29

3. Michael   37

Part 2

4. Michael   53

5. Tommaso Campanella   67

6. Leyla   81

Part 3

7. Leyla   99

8. Tommaso Campanella   109

9. Michael   125

Part 4

10. Michael   147

11. Tommaso Campanella   155

12. Leyla   159

Epilogue

13. Michael   171

14. Leyla   173

    Notes on Contributors   179

Illustrations

Thomas Eakins, *Female Nude from the Back*, ca. 1889.
Courtesy of the Metropolitan Museum of Art,
New York   5

Caravaggio, *The Musicians*, 1597. Courtesy of the
Metropolitan Museum of Art, New York   6

Thomas Eakins, *Thomas Eakins and John Laurie Wallace
on a Beach*, ca. 1883. Courtesy of the Metropolitan Museum
of Art, New York   51

Caravaggio, *The Seven Works of Mercy*, 1607. Courtesy of
Pio Monte delle Misericordia, Naples, Italy   52

Thomas Eakins, *Nude, Playing Pipes*, ca. 1883.
Courtesy of the Metropolitan Museum of Art,
New York   97

Caravaggio, *The Denial of Saint Peter*, 1610. Courtesy of the
Metropolitan Museum of Art, New York   98

Thomas Eakins, *Amelia Van Buren*, ca. 1880s.
Courtesy of the Metropolitan Museum of Art,
New York   145

Louis Finson or Caravaggio, *Judith Beheading Holofernes*,
1610, belonging to the Intesa Sanpaolo Collection.
Courtesy of the Archive, Art, Culture, and Historical
Heritage Head Office Department, Intesa Sanpaolo   146

Foreword

Caravaggio, Convergences, Craquelure

In today's English parlance, the word "syndrome" strikes a slightly pathologizing note—suggesting something that is suffered or diagnosed, the constellation of multiple symptoms into a single affliction.

Yet as the narrator of Alessandro Giardino's *The Caravaggio Syndrome* reminds us, by way of one protagonist's private musings, the word in its Greek origin denotes a "convergence," or more literally, a "running together." One of the word's striking early appearances in the English language—published just after Tommaso Campanella, another of the book's central figures, expired in the Parisian convent of Saint-Honoré—comes from the English medical reformer and alchemical author Noah Biggs, whose *Matæotechnia Medicinæ Praxeωs: The Vanity of the Craft of Physick* (1651) assails a "farraginous Syndrome of Knaves and Fools." This kind of invocation lends back to the term something of its earlier social, rather than merely symptomatic, resonance.

Giardino's title, at any rate, might be thought of as teasingly metonymical. For does not every novel enact a convergence of some sort, a running together of narrative threads—even if spun or strung at different angles, even if subsequently unraveled, even if never truly fully intertwined to begin with?

At first blush, *The Caravaggio Syndrome* seems to represent what we call a "campus novel." From Professor Leyla D'Andria's idyllic (if lonesome) perch on Saranac Lake and Saint Luke University, we travel with her back to various academic travails and triumphs, from the slog of a first job to the exaltation of promotion and tenure. Yet the novel swiftly opens up beyond the purview of professional pursuits, giving way to other subjects past and present, who animate its pages across geographies and temporalities.

As they converge and disperse and reappear in body or mind, we encounter Leyla's student, her lover, her student's lover, and the objects of her scholarly work—Michelangelo da Merisi, otherwise known as Caravaggio, and Tommaso Campanella, the philosopher, poet, and theologian whose confinement to Naples's prisons coincided with the legendary painter's exploits in the same city. Along with some of Campanella's contemporary and controversial texts, Caravaggio's allegorical altarpiece *The Seven Works of Mercy* (1607) emerges as a focal point around which the characters gravitate (at least mentally) and detach.

"Could a crack be enough to identify an artist, the nervous weakness that spreads from the soul to the hand?" thus muses Michael—one of the book's other protagonists—observing the small fissures in a painting by the eponymous seventeenth-century painter.

Even though a typology of cracks would never pass muster as a benchmark of art historical connoisseurship, the very notion conjures up questions about author and object, intention and effect, origins and afterlife, the singularity of meaning and the democratizing consequences of time. As much as iconography itself, this craquelure—as art historians call the web of fine fissures that spread out across the surface of a painting's dried oil (or the varnish used to seal it in place)— speaks to the sometimes talismanic pull of painting in general. Although it traces the symptoms of a specifically Caravaggian "syndrome," Giardino's novel pays homage to the enduring web of cracks and connections that certain paintings help us to grasp, well beyond their frames.

Ara H. Merjian
New York University

Translator's Note

Alessandro Giardino, the author of this unusual speculative novel, began speaking to me about his intentions at least a year before he even wrote a word. He spoke mostly about the twenty-first-century protagonist, Leyla, and her inordinate desire for a child. I had no idea that Tommaso Campanella, the seventeenth-century philosopher and Dominican friar, would loom so largely in the life of our heroine/art historian, plagued by her feelings of inadequacy toward her best-loved artist, Caravaggio, as well as toward every other human being in her life, including eventually her son. Not that we did not speak on many occasions about Campanella (we shared an office in the Italian Department at McGill University for many years), perhaps Alessandro's best-loved author at the time. And when I began to translate the novel, what a surprise to find within it Campanella's very own intimate diary, forged not in the soul of the friar himself but in the soul of our twenty-first-century wordsmith Alessandro. Merging the two stories together, that of the present-day art historian and her malaise and the philosopher of old and his malaise, was a veritable feat. Anyone interested in a writer's process—the way in which a creative mind works to meld the various and seemingly unrelated facets of a story—will surely be intrigued by the seamless flow from one century to another in this novel.

I am well aware that speculative fiction does not attract everyone. I have read the good and the bad. I have even translated fiction of that genre. But the artful way in which this author subtly and almost surreptitiously manages to incorporate elements from that genre will entice and satisfy the most stalwart of antagonistic readers. One just suspends disbelief and believes.

As a translator, moving from one era to another, from one linguistic modality to another, may seem to be a challenge (and I translated it the way it was written, not completing the contemporary story separately from the historical), but I have to say that I experienced no adverse impact to the transitions. I never recoiled and said to myself, "Hey, wait a minute! What is going on?" It was as if I were just ready for each metamorphosis. I wanted to hear each voice as it slithered into my consciousness.

My hope is that all readers of this novel (which, have no fear, is also about Caravaggio) will be effortlessly and smoothly carried along by its strange and century-jumping trajectory, just as I was.

Joyce Myerson

Author's Note

This novel has been such a marathon in translation. Indeed, it was not simply a question of translating a novel from Italian to English; well before that, it was about "whetting" the appetite of today's readers to seventeenth-century thinking, all the while pouring an emotional range that was mine into the psyches of complexly different characters.

When I first asked Joyce to help me bring this novel to an English-speaking audience, I knew this could get interesting. Not only was she familiar with the article on Caravaggio's painting I had published with Brill, "The Seven Works of Mercy: Love between Astrology and Natural Generosity in the Naples of Tommaso Campanella," but she was also a professional translator of medieval and early Renaissance texts from Italian to English. Moreover, I felt it was impossible to manage alone the linguistic boundaries of my particular idiolect—a mix of French, English, and literary Italian. In my view, her idiolect was just as much a mix of English, Italian, and French, yet—so to speak—it was an idiolect from the opposite side of the pond. And so the adventure began!

Our first dilemma was, of course, where to position ourselves on the spectrum between fidelity to the source text and enjoyability for the target audience. Having taught masterpieces of world literature in translation to several generations of students, I wanted a translation that would not completely obliterate the sound and feeling of a foreign language. Nevertheless, I did not want the pleasure of reading to be overwhelmed by odd-sounding and strange expressions steeped in another cultural heritage.

I knew Joyce could work well on the book's two linguistic registers, and I loved the idea that the inevitable choices of translations we had to make could be settled in a conversational fashion. What was even more fascinating in this case was that the process of translation had an impact on the source text itself, since the first draft in English was completed as I was finalizing the manuscript for my Italian publisher.

Then there was the issue of Campanella and his fictional journal, an issue characterized by the always imperfect compromise between a philologically accurate language, which risked aggravating readers, and on the other hand, a style of writing whose lack of credibility and excessive contemporaneity could have been equally off-putting and alienating. It would not do for Campanella to be uttering words derived from concepts or notions that had not yet appeared.

If any incongruence is noticed, I take the blame. And yet, I do suggest the reader not to jump to conclusions. Seventeenth-century thought is closer to ours than many scholars themselves know or acknowledge, and my fictional Campanella—as the reader would in time discover—is a character whose spiritual life exceeds the imprisoning boundaries of his own era.

In brief, the process of translation was as challenging and delightful as proofreading the numberless drafts in Italian. I could not have done it without Joyce and her magic wand.

And yet this was a Cinderella more demanding than others, as she made sure her new dress not to hinder the expediency of the dance. At the very end, rhythm was of the essence; the musicality had to be kept. And while some pauses and da capo repetitions will help reveal the deeper layers of the book, my sincere hope is that the reader will easily learn to move to the beat of my drum.

Alessandro Giardino

Preface

It was the winter of 1606 when Caravaggio arrived in Naples. He was escaping the judgment of capital punishment imposed on him after defending his honor. Once in the city, he painted *The Seven Works of Mercy*, an extraordinary altarpiece that would become a symbol of the city. During the same winter, Tommaso Campanella was serving the seventh of a twenty-seven-year jail sentence in the prisons of Sant'Elmo. He had been accused of conspiring and rebelling against the Spanish yoke as well as of heresy against the church of Rome. Yet, like a beacon of light from the pitch-black darkness of his cell, he would propagate revolutionary ideas about the universe, free love, and the power of the stars.

The Caravaggio Syndrome

Prologue

TOMMASO CAMPANELLA

My mother, Caterina Martello, died at the time when everyone called me Gian Domenico and I was timidly entering
my sixth year of life. That year hath remained linked by a
thin thread to my earlier childhood, one lived in total oblivion and then immediately forgotten. It is as if my life had
begun there and then, and it was only after her death that
my prophetic dreams began. Over the years, these dreams
have come more frequently and with greater clarity. My
mother's milk made me agile and slender, instilling in me a
worldly wisdom that made of me a connoisseur and master
of nature. Her absence opened up a chasm in my consciousness that allowed me, asleep, to gather voices and images
from centuries to come. There were days in which I hoped
my father would open up, reveal more about her, or at least
more than what he let slip so rarely. But he spent his days
shining shoes, tilling the soil. And as the seasons passed, that

life made him as wild as the wind and as irksome as the weeds. The appointment as mayor, and his pride in having being selected at least once in his life, seemed to afford him some respite as well as the desire to hold up his head, if only briefly. This period, however, passed quite quickly. But never could I blame or reprimand him, although later, when I was reborn as Tommaso Campanella, I did little else but disappoint him. His back broken by the daily grind, he forevermore fixed his gaze upon the earth. He often repeated these words: "The earth knows all, saith all." And to that earth, I myself often returned, not always by choice. Those years unwind like cotton wool, silent and soft in memory, because both sweetness and bitterness, impossible to recapture, lingered there together. I sometimes wonder if any of this ever really happened. I remember the throbbing in my spleen treated by a wood nymph by the light of the waning moon, the geometry lessons overheard from the school's courtyard— we lacked the money to have me attend—the mockery of the other children, and the rather harmless stones flung at me because of my knotted and misshapen brow. At times, this marginal life of mine brought me suffering, but it was not this childhood that made me who I am, that gave me the determination that would ultimately condemn me. What stung more than the cold of early morning was the pure unequivocal feeling that other terrible exiles awaited me, that everything would become greater, more painful. It was there, in the school's courtyard, where, hanging from a tree like a lizard, I called out loudly to Master Agazio who stood there so tiny in the back of the large hall: "I know the answer, sir! I know it! Can I say it?" Then, almost always, without waiting for his nod of approval, I would suddenly blurt out the answer, eliciting the ire of the teacher and the hilarity of his disciples. Since those days in the courtyard, many, too many years have passed, and those crystal-clear lessons of the teacher have been replaced by senseless discourses, endless absurdities even for those voicing them. Who are we? From where do we come? And what are the natural laws that sustain this world of ours? I write this diary so as not to take leave of my senses, because I struggle to see where this quest of mine will lead, because I have begun to fear . . . not so much for my life, which is in danger nonetheless, but for the inescapable obligation that binds us to the few true men of knowledge who have preceded us, and perhaps to those who will follow in our wake. I write, wracked by the anguish that once its direction is lost, truth will not find its way home. Blood is like a river that comes from elsewhere, flowing over infinite distances. Even before belonging to its progenitors, this blood of Dominic flowed through the veins of the Greeks who disembarked on Calabrian shores, refugees from deceit, survivors of an intolerable enslavement. I write so that blood may not lie.

PART 1

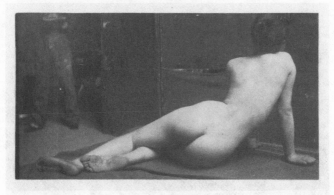

Thomas Eakins, *Female Nude from the Back*, ca. 1889.

Caravaggio, *The Musicians*, 1597.

~ 1 ~

Leyla

Saint Luke University, Saranac Lake,
New York—September 2006

It could be said that Leyla caused no small measure of apprehension in the residents of Saranac Lake, in her colleagues, as well as in those who considered themselves her friends. Many sensed uneasiness in her, a remoteness, an unsettling tension. However, no one had yet made the effort to probe into the why of her emotional wound. No one seemed to want to, and perhaps she herself had forgotten its causes. Leyla D'Andria was and indeed wished to be seen as a resolute and strong woman. She had come to Saint Luke University with all the pretensions and mannerisms of a girl born and brought up in Brooklyn by Italian-Turkish parents. And seldom did her small, round but slender body or her messy hair spark the sympathy of those few foreigners who, like her, floundered about like bewildered fish in a tiny bowl of water. When she was hired at Saint Luke University, Saranac Lake was a quiet rural community surrounded by pine trees and crossed by one of the hundred or so rivulets of the Saint Lawrence River separating the northeastern United States from the Canadian border. The university seemed like a cathedral in the desert to her since little remained of the late nineteenth-century Saranac Lake—a cheerful holiday resort—except for the quaint Victorian houses and the brick facades of the main street's businesses. Occasionally at night, Leyla would be woken up by her own screams, and this represented the only lingering sign that something was amiss. However, this alarming expression of agitation would soon be drowned out by the whistle of the train that passed through the village every four hours, as precise as a Swiss cuckoo clock. This was a train that, because of the financial collapse of the 1920s and the dismantling of the American railway system, sped through Saranac Lake without ever stopping, thus relegating the town to a cocoon-like isolation and forever adding insult to injury in the eyes of the town's residents.

When Leyla walked, her back was slightly bowed, her eyes on the ground, lending an observer the impression that she was in a hurry. Little did the observer know that Leyla, for no apparent reason, sincerely believed that she was always late. In fact, on this morning toward the end of September, she was once again in a hurry as she lunged forward, slightly limping, toward the Visual Arts Department, her wide hips swaying on her scrawny birdlike legs. It's not that she expected to find any students or colleagues waiting for her. She was always the first to arrive, and she was well aware of the fact that after winning her self-inflicted race, she would end up inevitably sitting and staring at the empty corridor stretching before her. And this occurred day after day. There was always a lesson to prepare, some paperwork to organize, a book to review, an essay to correct. However, for over a month, the article she was writing on the subject of *Salome* in seventeenth-century Neapolitan painting had lain unfinished and slowly dying among the other papers on her desk. She wondered, "What demon could have possibly possessed me to dedicate myself to Caravaggio and his copiers?" And along with this thought, she began to recall the fables her grandmother used to tell her over the course of the long, torrid summers spent in Istanbul, fables of unhappy princesses, of moons trapped in well water, and of jinn capable of seducing and manipulating even the most virtuous of knights. These were tales that spoke of her origins and clashed with the label "American" that cousins and relatives sprang on her, revealing that somewhere, deep inside, there lay a warrior armed with a scimitar, a Scheherazade-like storyteller, fighting for her life. Yet, some-how, those summers had already begun to decay like the rotten fruit of her fierce imagination. And in all honesty, she had to admit that running around in circles helped her to breathe, prevented her from being overwhelmed by the thick swamp of her painful past . . . and more importantly of her present, riddled with danger and humiliation.

University of Arizona, Tucson, Arizona—
September 2005, One Year Earlier...

When Leyla accepted the position at the University of Arizona, she was attracted by the promise of the sweeping desert, the dream of warmth in the morning, and by the fact that since she had received no other offer of employment after finishing her doctorate, what else was she to do? In Arizona, life would probably be more monotonous but less expensive. Also, she had told herself that with a little bit of luck, she would meet a handsome southerner, with skin the color of leather and hair the color of straw—a gentleman cowboy with whom to make love twice a week and raise four children, preferably boys. Unfortunately, as soon as classes were underway, she did not have a moment's peace. She had to conjure up lesson plans out of thin air, prepare exams, and attend, participate in, and even organize meeting after meeting. Students were so relentless in sending her emails that she felt besieged and powerless to find even a minute to devote to herself. The dean's office pushed for bigger classes: groups of fifty, even a hundred students. She found herself correcting avalanches of student papers, her work becoming a constant, Promethean, and— as it happened—completely futile task. Three years slipped by in a whirlwind, without a whiff of that southern gentleman. She was thirty-eight years old. She felt dull and drab. Not that she was imagining going the route of IVF to create a family, but she mused, if along came a decent civil servant in lieu of the cowboy and if he got her pregnant and stopped by every now and then, maybe raising a child on her own would not be that strenuous. In the meantime, her never-ending work assignments remained the major obstacle to the fulfillment of any personal goal or aspiration, be it even the simple act of painting her nails. Notwithstanding this, between doing the laundry and grading a stack of essays over the course of an autumn weekend, Leyla found the time to sit down at her backyard table and fill out a couple of job applications.

Nothing and no one could have predicted what would happen next, but the mere fact that a morning's rain had interrupted the unbearable Arizona heat of the last few weeks made Leyla mutter almost aloud, "No torture lasts forever." However, upon arriving at her doorstep, the rain beating down on her, she came to realize her keys were still in the office, most probably on her desk. She admonished herself for the premature celebration of victory, and after a detour back to the office, she returned to her front door, only to find a letter from Saint Luke University. It was an invitation to a job interview for a position in Renaissance art, the position for which she had applied at least a month prior. Wasn't it a little late for such an invitation? Did she read it correctly? The letter mentioned that the interview would take place in early January at a national conference in Boston and that "unfortunately" no refund for travel and accommodation expenses could be expected. Upon a quick calculation of prices, Leyla felt her heart sink. The cost of the trip would be astronomical. And yet, how could she possibly reject such an offer? She had just spent month after month bemoaning her current working conditions, and all things considered, she could not imagine anything more thrilling than an escape to Boston. What would Boston be like in winter? Whom would she meet? Leyla imagined the long downtown boulevards blanketed in snow, a snow that sneaked under doorways like a thick carpet. She hoped that Boston could inspire a better version of herself, a more elegant and mature woman, a less disheveled Leyla, at least for a couple of days. Maybe the city's energy would infect her like a virus that meets no resistance. A sense of contentment and tranquility was welling up within her. And then, all of a sudden, her stomach lurched and a shrill cry escaped her lips. She doubled over, as an image from her past resurfaced and obliterated that laboriously constructed self-portrait of success, thus threatening her already precarious stability. In particular, what emerged from her hidden depths was an obscene yet banal memory, an incident without significance. Because, after all, what did that limp penis signify? What was the meaning of that nudity glimpsed by the little girl behind a bathroom door left ajar as she wandered the rooms of the house looking for her father? She knew very well that it was her fault and hers alone if that image had flashed before her eyes for little more than a second, if it had left its mark. But why this pain, then? Why this unexpected ache inside her woman's body on the threshold of forty? And why was this memory resurfacing now? Still in the throes of her anguish, she comforted herself with a platitude: it must be the stress of the upcoming interview, the usual anxiety. In the meantime, her cell phone, lying on the table, had started to ring, but Leyla, as if stuck to the kitchen stool, could not seem to rally herself to reach it. Finally, on all fours, she crawled toward it.

"Leyla, it's me, Grandma!"

"Hi, Grandma. Everything all right? What's up?"

"Leyla, in case you didn't know, your grandma is still alive. You could make a phone call once in a while."

Leyla had no idea how to answer her. And what's more, having just managed to haul her body up, she had little or no strength to react, let alone defend herself. But her grandmother did not pause. She just changed her tone, as if changing gears, and softly added, "You're working too much, aren't you? You're always busy, just like your father." Then, "On another note, have you found a boyfriend yet—a partner? Leyla, you have to get a move on. Listen to your grandma!"

The conversation continued along these lines, between scolding and cajoling, for about twenty minutes, after which Leyla hastily promised to call more often and hung up. Immediately afterward—totally lost in thought—she continued to stare at the phone. She imagined her grandma clasping her handset like a rodent. She thought of the dark and cramped New York apartment she had purchased in her old age so as to be closer to her children and grandchildren—an apartment so different from her airy villa on the Bosporus, where the scent of tulips and hydrangeas mingled with the stronger aroma of *hünkar beğendi* and of the ubiquitous sticky-sweet honey. Revisiting in her mind the summers she had spent there in childhood, Leyla remembered how, as soon as she stepped into the kitchen, her grandma (without even a hello) would instantly hand her a chopping board or a pot. It was at that time that the injustices began. But then, in hindsight, Leyla would ask herself if she had not been right to tolerate the constant barrage of unreasonable demands and abuses on the part of whomever: colleagues, friends, students, and yes, even her grandmother. Mostly, she regretted not having been able to latch on to a concept of love that could help her survive every privation, mistreatment, and violence. Nor could she manage to throw off that dreaded statement, "You're just like your father, her favorite." She would ask herself, "Aren't favorite children supposed to be the meekest, the most subdued, those who read in every parental gesture an invitation to be accommodating and cooperative?" The painful image of the half-opened door fleetingly came to mind before slowly vanishing into the deep well of memory. Now she felt nothing. At most, what lingered was an irritation, a sense of disappointment, a barely perceptible longing . . . for what exactly, she could not say.

And so Leyla began to contemplate anew her grandmother, Perla De Andria. She especially spent time brooding over the childhood of the old woman in an Istanbul that was then known as Constantinople, but she also tried to imagine the relationship of Perla with *her* own father, whose surname she would eventually decide to keep. Having been brought up in the Levantine community of the city by a man who considered himself more Venetian than Italian and "not one iota Turkish" (a phrase she often accompanied by a movement of the brow that indicated a sentiment between sarcasm and nostalgia), Perla was only seventeen when she had abandoned her Galata neighborhood, followed her Muslim hotelkeeper of a husband, and broke the heart of the father for whom the Ottoman would eternally represent the enemy. Having then moved to the ground floor of the Grand Hotel Paradise in the central district of Sultanahmet—the two rooms in which they lived could only be accessed through reception—Perla had just given birth to two perfectly healthy sons when her husband took off to the other world and happily joined the virgins and the fruit trees promised him by his Koran. Left alone, Leyla's grandmother had then decided to reclaim her paternal surname and fully commit to her children: Okan, the elder, to whom she would later entrust the management of the hotel, and Erkan, her darling (and later, father to Leyla), with whom she would move to the legendary villa on the Bosporus, and from there to the Lower East Side. How Erkan ever managed to free himself from the clutches of this colossal mother and find a wife remained to this day a mystery to Leyla. The fact was that between vengeful Italian roots, absent fathers, and symbolic castrations, a certain amount of psychological ill health was bound to emerge.

Boston, Massachusetts—January 2006: First Interview for Saint Luke University

She walked toward the location of the interview with the stride of a model and the heart of a criminal about to face a firing squad. Everything was a matter of life and death with her, everything final and definitive. She was mindful of the fact that coming into the interview with another job in hand constituted a practical advantage. She would be considered a colleague, the honorary member of a very "exclusive" club. And yet, something was bothering her, a sensation that was making her feel anxious but alive for the first time in months. Once she was in front of the door, she looked at her watch, knocked, and entered the hotel room designated as the interview space. A minute later, she was speaking with three strangers who were scrutinizing her with befuddled expressions, nodding mechanically at her every response. "What are you currently working on? How do you think you can use your research over the course of the first year? What changes have you made to your dissertation in order to develop it into a book?" It all lasted about twenty minutes at the most—a barrage of formulaic questions—which she answered as if in a trance. The Leyla watching her from the outside seemed to want to stop the other, that voracious, uninhibited, cannibal-like Leyla. Nevertheless, when, at 11:35 A.M., she exited the conference room, the two Leylas came together, and without any need for explanation, walked hand in hand toward her hotel room, one body alone on the move: a tired body, however, tired of everything.

Back in her room, Leyla realized that she had to stop moving at least for a moment. It had been months, maybe years, since she had stretched out on a bed without immediately beginning to enumerate the things to be done, to organize, to decide on. Instead, the only obligation she had to fulfill in Boston was this interview. Now that it was over, she felt completely liberated: free to do anything but mostly to do nothing. She looked at her stomach, which was slightly plumper than it had been at twenty. The stress of the courses, the absence of time, the incessant demands of students had

caused her to gain weight as if she had been in a hydropho-
bic state. Lying on the linen sheets, her arms limp and inert,
she felt like the protagonist of a tableau vivant, and it occurred
to her that perhaps the unhappy heroine of Caravaggio's
Death of the Virgin had experienced the same sensations as
she was feeling and that perhaps it was why the meaning of
the painting continued to elude her. In truth, every time she
had to explain to her students the reason for that bulge in
the stomach of the Virgin, she found herself inventing some
new interpretation. One time, it was because the artist had
chosen for a model a prostitute who had drowned in the
Tiber. Another time, the artist had wanted to represent the
"Madonna full of Grace." On other occasions, she had talked
about a sick woman, or she had referred to a model who had
not yet given birth. Each reason made Caravaggio seem like
a heretical and unorthodox painter. But could it be that this
early seventeenth-century Madonna in the painting was a
little overly plump, perhaps just a woman with an appetite,
because food was the only thing that made her feel full, in
the absence of love, in the anticipation of a son? And while
she pondered these inconclusive theories, two tears slipped
down her cheeks. For the first time, she realized how much
she wanted a child, a child to call her own. She abruptly
raised herself, threw on her coat, headed out the door, and
into the snowy streets of Boston. She needed air; she hoped
for food.

University of Arizona, Tucson, Arizona—
March 2006: After the First Interview

The return flight from Boston had been an uninterrupted
ordeal of turbulence, but perhaps the nausea she experienced during the trip could not be blamed on the bouncing

and jolting of the plane alone. Returning to teach in Arizona—after hustling to be hired elsewhere—had made her feel like a cheating wife sneaking into the marriage bed after a night of dissolute passion. She felt dirty, worn out, and sadly apathetic. Nothing would ever be like it once was. And although she tried to convince herself that deep down, she liked her current job, that "the show must go on," a little voice was telling her that no, she aspired to something more, yearned for a different life, that after five gruesome hours of turbulence, all that emotional struggle in the end had lost any meaning. After a few days, however—also thanks to an innate predisposition to accept whatever life threw at her— Leyla calmed down. Giving up this alternate destiny helped her to accept her present with a modicum of wisdom and grace. The freckles that had appeared on her face (she was ten years old on the beach of Kemer the last time they had so conspicuously exploded) were perhaps a sign of that rediscovered lightheartedness. More unusual and sinister, on the other hand, had been the snowfall that covered Arizona at the end of winter. Only a delicate powder, to be sure, yet enough to send her students into a frenzy. Leyla was terrified by it. It had filled her with a terror similar to the kind of feeling she might have felt had she been stalked by a maniac. In her mind, it was as if a trail of blood had inched its way between Boston and her present, and only she could see its opalescent stains. She was overwhelmed by an irrational shame, like the shame of one's first menstruation. Luckily, twenty-four hours later, the hot southern wind swept away the traces of a past too short to generate real consequences and, with the wind, the security of a tiresome but bearable routine. She was content with her professional situation, maybe even with her life. So the letter that summoned her to Saint Luke University for a final interview and a visit to the campus hit her like a shocking jolt of electricity.

What to say? What to wear? She was sure that the tone with which she chose to express herself, as much as a successful combination of purse and shoes, would constitute the only criteria of judgment on the part of the selection committee. When she was still pursuing her doctorate, she had had the opportunity to observe the performances of various candidates for similar positions. Invariably, regardless of the long and elaborate presentations on their research, of their experience teaching, of the publications lined up on their résumés like so many little boats in the marina, on every single occasion, it was the candidates' shoes and briefcase or purse, as well as a particular sense of confidence conveyed by their speech and movement that had been the determining factors in their getting hired. She recalled one of her first interviews in London for a position, which she thought to be unattainable but which instead, once she had met the other two candidates in the waiting room, she had believed was possibly within her grasp. During their brief exchange, in fact, she had noted how the two academics, already in their forties, both betrayed their working-class background in their accent and tone of voice but also in the elegance of their appearance, which, extravagant in every detail, demonstrated by and large their financial limitations. So she had rejoiced, unbeknownst to them, having determined that whatever they said and did, they would only ever obtain little more than the compassion of the committee. But then, *she* suddenly arrived on the scene: Catherine—blonde, slender, with one of those long compound surnames evoking the aristocratic lineage of ancient landed gentry. She had greeted everyone with the grace and delicacy of a winner. For Leyla, the interview was over in that moment. Over time, she had become savvier. She knew that her work in Arizona had enhanced the value of her "academic capital," that all she had to do was display her beauty and indifference—in other words, to do as little as possible, and this new position could be hers. And then what? What would happen afterward? She would still be a woman on her own, attractive for a little while and then invisible for much longer. She would live at the border with Canada instead of the border with Mexico, and that geographic location would remind her that regardless of every move and permutation, there would always be a threshold that remained insurmountable. "It's ridiculous to get depressed over something you're powerless to change," she silently concluded with a shrug. "It makes more sense to get ready for the interview." Such a pity that all she could manage to focus on were the semitransparent silk dress hanging over the chair and her super-high-heeled black shoes—"the shoes of a young widow" was the phrase that came to mind, "the footwear of a she-wolf in a negligee."

As she was filling her leather suitcase, she remembered how she had found it by chance in her mother's closet several years ago, immediately falling in love with it. It was inexplicably heavy even when empty and had threadbare handles. Yet Leyla continued to randomly throw things into it, as if it were a trunk in which one hid stuff from around the house just before guests were to arrive for a party. She also threw in a copy of *The City of the Sun* by Tommaso Campanella. She was hoping that it could shed some light on seventeenth-century Naples as well as on the courtesans and noblewomen who had inspired so many paintings like *Salome*. So, as she searched in her drawers for her best lingerie, she chuckled to herself, imagining that during the course of the interview, they might ask her to undress and perform a dance of the seven veils. She dallied about wondering whether it was preferable to wear comfortable underwear or something more daring, but eventually the idea of spending twelve, thirteen hours in a skimpy thong seemed more idiotic than anything else. Slowly, her smile transformed into a bitter frown: participating in a job interview to feel seductive was the ultimate proof of her existential degeneration, of the debasement into which she had been sinking as of late. But then, she took heart: after all, it had been on the occasion of a job interview that she had enjoyed an evening of sex the last time. Over the course of one night, Raoul, a super endowed doctoral candidate, almost ten years her junior, had caused her to envision a new season of sexual exploits, the dispersing of the clouds. Obviously, nothing of the sort had materialized, and the episode had been the proverbial swallow that does not a summer make. But while she was thinking all this, in an unusual state of erotic excitement and exhilaration, an abrupt abdominal spasm knocked her to the floor. This time, it occurred in two stages: at first with a slight warning punch, then with a harder blow, similar to a knife stab in her side. Never before had she been hurt so violently. Lying on the ground, like a bird brought down by a bullet, Leyla counted the minutes: one, two, three, four. . . . Then she counted again. They were like the slow-motion beats of a floundering heart, but they continued to throb relentlessly, beyond time, beyond her body, until the pain passed, slowly, like an exsanguination, like the night awaiting her beneath the leaden April sky. She understood that her sleep would be agitated, as on the occasions just before a trip or on that night when, as a little girl, she had slept in her parents' bed, her wet bathing suit clinging to her.

Saint Luke University, Saranac Lake,
New York—November 2006

When had she received the job offer from Saint Luke University? When had she first inserted the keys into the door
of the small two-story cottage provided by the Office of
Human Resources? It was already three and a half months
since she had first arrived in Saranac Lake, and it seemed as
if only a few hours had passed since that first day. It also
meant that it was more than three months since she had finished her article on the subject of *Salome* and had begun
work on her paper on Caravaggio's *The Seven Works of Mercy*.
Truth be told, she had not yet accomplished a single thing.
She often wondered whether it was worth plugging away at
it. And yet, every time she examined the painting again, she
became enthralled by the figure of the girl, who, willful and
unkempt, offers her breast to the old man in chains. Still, she
could not say whether the girl's face was stricken by a sense
of duty, by the fear of being discovered, or by another unfathomable tribulation, a nascent madness. She would automatically turn her gaze to the face of the old man—subdued,
pathetic, and quick to abdicate all dignity to survive and be
nourished. And what if, she thought, the excuse of hunger
served only to satisfy a craving that would be considered
offensive in other circumstances? She would have liked to
know whether, among the seventeenth-century patrons, there
were those who found that detail awkward, distasteful,
unacceptable. Those patrons were all men, but even so, they
would have had mothers, daughters, sisters. But then, she
concluded, the answer to the question was there in front of
everyone. The painting had not been moved from the high
altar of the Pio Monte for over four hundred years. Every

centimeter of it, however uncomfortable, had been repeatedly reproduced and copied, without a twinge of remorse. In her case, then, she could not hide a certain amount of turmoil, and not so much because the desperate gesture of that woman had become a metaphor for Christian charity but because it was an admission of denied motherhood, because there was no trace of the baby who made her a nursing mother. She had been researching and writing for the last three months, but that detail was the thorn in her side, the tether that held her back—her stumbling block. Inside her, there was a little girl kicking and screaming, but she didn't know what that girl wanted from her mature self. And in the meantime, where was her mother?

One Month Later

They had met at an end-of-semester party organized by the university, and in that moment, Leyla hadn't had the courage to ask him for which department he worked, not having remembered if she had seen him at a faculty meeting. However, she soon intuited that Pablo was not part of the teaching staff. His fleshy lips (almost like a woman's, she thought), his bronzed and somewhat spotty complexion, and those bowed legs like those of a soccer player or menial worker did not speak of higher learning. He was too humble, too servile, too much of a nice guy to nurture any academic aspirations. On the contrary, she had immediately found him irritating. Why did he feel obliged to fawn over anyone who paid him the slightest attention? And what was the meaning of that constant waving, that running from one end of the room to the other to refill someone's glass of wine or cut a piece of cake for someone else? She would have liked to stop him, help him regain his dignity, shake him, but here he was, moving in on her with the broadest of smiles, showing all his pearly whites.

"May I offer you a glass of wine?" he asked.

"Well, since you've already offered one to almost everyone else . . ."

"Let's say that I'm offering you the best glass or, since there is only one bottle left, the fullest glass," said Pablo with a wink.

"You really know how to make a woman feel special," answered Leyla, a bit peeved.

After some small talk, she learned that Pablo was a computer technician, that he worked at the university part time, and that he wished for nothing better because as he boastingly admitted, "I like to sleep in." In the meantime, she realized that she had already fallen into the trap, the one in which the bitter woman of a certain age promptly falls for men with no prospects—that is, men in need of guidance and improvement. Then, just as in the tritest of soap operas, Pablo escorted her home and she invited him in. It took no more than a few seconds before they threw themselves at each other like animals—against the wall, on the floor. They tumbled about everywhere except on the bed, where—she shuddered—she hadn't changed the sheets in months. Right then and there, she felt younger, fitter. Afterward, she wondered why Pablo hadn't even tried to approach the bed. What was the problem? Ultimately, however, she didn't really care that much. After months of abstinence, she didn't choose to delve into it too deeply. And then she asked herself, "Was it really so bad if she was only interested in him physically?" Experience had taught her that once illusions had been dispelled, all men were more or less the same; better to see the truth for what it was right away. She had her books, her work, her friends to talk to. Pablo would represent the missing piece. He would help her to complete the puzzle of an otherwise satisfying life. Were it not for the fact that once completed, the image it displayed was totally wrong, an aberration fashioned by chance. The pieces had been assembled together, true enough, but randomly and according to some abstruse logic. "I have everything and I'm dissatisfied," she ruefully reflected. Then, sighing, she silently added, "At least I can pour my dissatisfaction into this stranger." In fact, even though Pablo in no way represented the panacea she so longed for, he made her feel good, as only a scapegoat knows how to do. And so, as Leyla's frustration increased, their sexual encounters became more aggressive, rougher. She was convinced that Pablo discussed her with his good-for-nothing friends, that he described her as a lustful sexual partner, and that she aroused and satisfied him. They were sure to find it quite hilarious that a bespectacled professor was a more enthusiastic lover than the girls their age. And even if there were days in which she felt demoralized by the wall of incomprehension growing higher and higher between them, Pablo was, and continued to be, her perfect lover. Ten years her junior but capable of the dedication of an older man, he was generous in the bedroom as only men without ambition know how to be. Leyla knew little of him or of his past in the Peruvian community from which he hailed. One thing she knew though: in spite of his inherited defects and the miracles his single mother had worked on him, every time, after she had reached an orgasm, she really couldn't stand him. In those moments, she felt an instinctive disgust for this partner without prospects, for his unctuousness, and she was overcome by a blind hatred, not only for him but for the entire male gender.

She had repeated the pregnancy test three, four times. She knew the results were unequivocal, but if only she were able to deceive the test just once, maybe her body would follow suit and free her from this disaster. It saddened her to think that there wasn't a lonelier woman than one who—although wishing for a child her entire life, at first unconsciously and then driven by a relentless desire—becomes a mother but is unable to share the joys of motherhood with anyone, not even herself. And yet, this was not the moment to be overwhelmed by rage over an unwanted pregnancy or by bitterness over a destiny that, instead of giving her a life partner, foisted on her a dolt of a dad. She had to move fast, prepare for whatever was going to come hurtling down on her. It was especially necessary to figure out how to manage Pablo, what to tell him, and above all, how to get rid of him. Perhaps in the absence of a father, the child could still be saved. Perhaps upbringing could win out over genes. She felt as if she were losing her mind. She was aware of the fact that at this rate, the article that she had in mind would never be written and that, probably, the only sensible thing that she had done in the last few months was to have asked Michael, one of her brighter students, to complete a paper on the figure of the Madonna in Neapolitan painting. With a little outside help, she could gingerly recover her equilibrium and proceed with her research. Could she also ask Michael, this timid and unsuspecting student of hers, to take the bull by the horns and pound her passionately and unrelentingly into the ground? She felt as if she were observing herself outside her body, wondering who on earth this reckless and ruthless woman she encountered in the mirror was.

Where had she been hiding, and from where did she come? Sometimes self-knowledge was an excuse for not looking deeper inside.

She was hanging some of her skirts in her closet and looking at them in disbelief, thinking that in time, she would not be able to fit into them. Then an unexpected feeling of happiness overtook her: a new life was growing inside of her. She wondered, as she felt it move within, if she was making it up? She wanted to protect that life from every depravity of the flesh, from every error to which her failed childhood had unwittingly driven her. She recalled again the Caravaggio painting, *The Seven Works*, and began to wonder whether the Madonna with her child at the top, near the frame, was also a survivor. Had she fled a violent or unsuitable husband? Had she been forced to find refuge in the dark alleyways of seventeenth-century Naples? And then, pausing to rest at a street corner, did she perhaps see sense in the sermons of the young Tommaso Campanella, this unknown Dominican friar, who, in his disquisitions on uterine life, ascribed to women the role of sole genetrix? Probably the woman in the picture did not understand much of these theories, but rightly or wrongly, she had grasped that this child had to be hers and hers alone. Then again, it seemed to Leyla that it was always like this with Caravaggio. Every detail of a painting opened a gateway into another universe. Each protagonist was tangled up in a story that belonged to him or her alone. Until, upon observing them a little longer, these same protagonists began to manifest symptoms of one particular illness, an inner disease that drove them toward the epicenter of the representation, as if toward a black hole. Perhaps that was the fate of the poor woman whom the painter had designated as a Madonna of the people. And perhaps a similar fate had befallen Tommaso Campanella and the many friends gravitating toward him at the time that *The Seven Works* came to light. As a matter of fact, on rereading Campanella's books, which she carried everywhere like amulets, Leyla had lingered on that fateful year, 1607, in which Caravaggio, already sentenced to death, had been received in Naples by the same young men that Campanella was secretly teaching from his prison. She recalled that the word "syndrome" in Greek meant "convergence." And so she wondered if, besides poring over texts and iconographies, she should try to reassemble the fragments that had made up that scene, describing the manner of their convergence, and whether, instead of techniques and connotations, it wasn't simply better to just call it what it was: a syndrome, a Caravaggio syndrome.

~ 2 ~

Tommaso Campanella

Nicastro, the Kingdom of Naples—October 1586

I have been lodging for about two months at the Convent of the Annunziata in Nicastro, a place that represents the third educational phase of a novitiate that began in Placanica and, geographically speaking, is an additional fold in this mysterious stretch of the Apennines. I have thus found, within these sometimes barren, sometimes luxuriant mountains, a slight solace, a lair in which to lie low and renew my energy while awaiting new challenges, a bower in which to devote myself to my beloved authors. I am still grateful to my father who hath desisted in the notion of making me a man of the law. Originally, he had decided to direct me to my uncle Julius in Naples, a jurist of the court. However, the life of hardship to which we Calabrians are forced to suffer in the capital of the kingdom, as well as the recent prohibition to avoid penury through private lessons, would have rendered any attempt of mine to study if not futile, at the very least frustratingly difficult. It was this same uncle who might dissuade him. Here, on the other hand, sheltered from the city and from its temptations as well as from its exorbitant costs, I had the opportunity to reread the writings of Aristotle from cover to cover. I did it to quell those doubts that have hounded me for quite some time. I did not overlook anything. I worked systematically, examining thoroughly each and every passage. I was determined to "rejoin the ranks," as urged by various fathers superior I have known. Unfortunately, this reading enterprise did nothing but yield the opposite effect by opening new and irreparable fissures, further undermining my faith in the Aristotelian system. Initially, I read Aristotle's commentators, and I lingered over the passages translated into Latin or Arabic without finding any validation therein. And so, I resolved to look into Plato, Galen, the Stoics but especially Democritus and his followers. I chastised myself: If everyone argues the contrary of what thou believe to see, then it's thou who errs, thou who lacks knowledge, thine eye that is mistaken. Notwithstanding this, the more I delved into my study of those writings, the more a painful fear made its way into me. I passed sleepless nights skipping from text to commentary, from commentary to other translations, and on no occasion did I gain enlightenment or knowledge. It was during those nights that I began to have dreadfully disturbing dreams.

At first, I thought I was having brief hallucinations or hazy fantasies, precursors to the languor of sleep. But they were bewildering dreams, intrauterine visions. I felt as if I were enclosed within the body of a woman. I sensed the hand of a mother on me like a cloud in the sky since in that moment, everything grew darker and I was seized by a painful heat and by the physical agony of that woman carrying me in her womb. Sometimes it was as if I heard the woman intone refrains similar to the litanies of infidels; at other times, the uterus contracted, forcing me to recoil; less often, from very far off, I heard a different voice, a male voice. It was through the voice of that man, however, that I learned the name of the future mother—Leyla—pronounced in a hybrid accent, made up of incomprehensible vowels. And yet, at each one of those cries, a timid smile would creep over my face.

Naples, the Kingdom of Naples—Three Years Later

The year 1589 marcheth on. Under the cover of night, Abraham and I have finally reached Naples. In fact, while in Cosenza, our relationship had caused too much of an uproar. We could not stay in Calabria, lest the bitterness of the brothers of Altamonte be unleashed on us. They envied our astrological knowledge. They disparagingly called us necromancers. They could not accept that a simple Jew like Abraham could speak with their dead. On the other hand, Abraham himself did nothing to suppress these suspicions and jealousies. In reality, from the moment the people of the county began to listen to him, and perhaps blinded by the love he felt toward me, he began to prophesize that Campanella would become king of the world. At any rate, our flight from Calabria toward the capital had nothing kingly about it. I entered Naples by the Capuana Gate, and since my entrance, the city hath seemed more crowded, more suffocating, and poorer than I was told. I cannot deny that wandering through the center, continuously stepping over a carpet of corpses, hath generated in me a mental weariness that pursues me late into the night. I look around me, trying to push away a persistent sensation of danger. Here in Naples, it's practically impossible to take two steps without being followed by a thousand sets of eyes or without being pulled by little rascals, who, like rats, crawl out of every corner and scurry into every alleyway. The beggars rant and rave, eyes wide open like vultures, and the women, by day hardworking and devoted mothers, by nightfall have all become ravenous prostitutes. It is difficult not to feel guilt about my own scant wealth and not to show indignation for a government over which no one in the city seems to fret. And yet, somewhere between fear and discomfort, I am quite happy to have become part of a group of like-minded souls, young aristocrats determined to correct the errors of their fathers, scholars hungry for renewal . . . or at least that is the hope! In the past, I already had the opportunity to observe how the palingenetic enthusiasms of youth doth not last more than one spring season, sadly dying into dust at the first swish of a skirt. By virtue of the intervention of a noblewoman, I was invited to stay at the home of Mario Tufo, one of these young men. In fact, it had been difficult to find a spot at the Convent of Saint Dominic, despite the occasional availability that the nocturnal rampages of the brothers between taverns and bordellos should have afforded. And so here I am, welcomed in an excellent and unexpected residence on Via Santa Maria di Costantinopoli, while, thanks to Mario and his friend Orazio Salviano, I obtained the resources and courage with which to publish my *Philosophy Demonstrated by the Senses*, a work that cost me many sleepless nights during the isolation that Altomonte forced on me. Hence the teachings of Telesius will find in Naples their first home. For my part, it behooveth me to strive so that his message may be carried from here to the ends of the earth. Moreover, if a regret for having posthumously met this master resides in me *ad aeternum*—a regret for having arrived too late, late by a day and then by another—I would like to be sure that Telesius, in his infinite wisdom, died knowing that Campanella would have carried his teachings far and wide. At his tomb, speaking no longer to his body but to whatever was left of his immortal soul still entangled within the luminous mortal remains, I promised that science and reason would become my sole reason for living. So it would be. So it is already.

Here in Naples, I have come into possession of writings subject to censorship, and thanks to the safe haven that the Tufo family provided me, I am devouring the pages therein, without however being able to satiate my profound hunger; and the more of them that I finish and add to the pile, the more voracious becomes my craving to read those still awaiting me. I often reprimand myself, "Enough! Thou have consumed too many already!" But these admonishments last only seconds, and then I feel as if I am dying of starvation. Besides which, the hours passed in reading offer me the necessary calm to tolerate the injuries and provocations of those who, like Del Marta, dishonor truth and justice for political gain. Alas, we live in a dictatorship of the single thought. The Aristotelians like Del Marta, with their heavy, dark, and bilious spirits, are everywhere. And this is why the world around us reeks! The groans of these fetid pigs cover the truth that shines within Telesius's simplicity. One law, instead, governs all that exists within the universe, within our lives, and even within this confession of mine, and this law affirms: on the one hand, there is the heat and the fire and the love that sets everything in motion; on the other hand is the cold that restrains and obstructs, the cold that saith, wait, try again, try later.

Recently, I dreamed of a trial and then another and another one again. There were long hallways in which lights and shadows alternated like in the ancient caves of the Sibyls: in bright light were my jailers, in the shadow, older images of ropes, rafters, and torture wheels. I had a vivid dream of the last day in the life of Giordano Bruno, whose feet I glimpsed on the stake. Only in a later moment did I see his face engulfed by flames, and yet this time, the image was less recognizable. In fact, what I saw crackling in the fire was not a man but a wet piece of wood, an ember, a heap of ashes. It was in another vision, then—I am not sure how removed from my first one—that my interminable captivity as well as my subsequent life presented themselves once more to me. On this occasion, however, I did not see the pitch-black night and the snug chamber of the maternal womb. In its place, there was now a glaring light, the terrifying and shocking feeling of a freefall. I said to myself that it was my entry into the world, the blinding of the prisoner on the day of his release, and as a blind person, his being hurled toward an alien planet where wild beasts roam. And then, the face of Leyla.

Rome, the Papal States—May 1592

"Possessed by the devil, bile runs through his veins and with it a knowledge too vast, and therefore suspect." These were the arguments gathered by the inquisitors of the Holy Office against me, and though rambling and disjointed, they seemed to be enough to mount a trial. Placed in chains and forcibly conducted from Naples to Rome, I thus had to defend myself from those accusations but also from additional inferences associated with a pair of sentences pronounced by me on the church forecourt of Saint Dominic and then cunningly recorded and reported by "friends" to the authorities. My real friends attribute this to envy and old grudges. Alas, I fear that it is simply stubbornness. In actuality, my knowledge appeared suspect because, in my little corner of the world, it was not old wines like Falanghina or Lacryma Christi that was plenteously flowing, but the liters of the midnight oil I have burned, poring over my papers. "His sentences are abstruse!"—they added—"He brazenly shows off his bottomless repository of knowledge." Well, if one is guilty of diabolical possession for having soaked up learning from Jews, Turks, and Aryans, one would be forced to conclude that the devil recruited many followers in this instance. However, more than the accusations, what unduly grieves me is this dread of mine: the dread of prison and, even more, that of an ignominious death. My associates repeat that these are frivolous accusations, that it will all end up as inconsequential as a soap bubble since it is laughable to think that senseless arguments have the strength to extinguish a human life. But how not to think of the recent arrest of Giordano Bruno in Venice? Could he have predicted that the impossible, because invoked, would become reality? Certainly, we, his friends, didn't predict it while we were spending long afternoons around the hundred-year-old medlar tree of Stigliola. And I certainly had not imagined it in the period when we were all meeting at the home of the Della Porta brothers in Piazza Carità, that residence of theirs that had already become a mecca for magicians and astrologers from all over Europe. The stream of inquisitive minds that roamed the corridors of this house had, in fact, perpetuated in us the illusion that the century on our doorstep would sweep away the shadows of ignorance and parade the triumph of free thinkers. And to convince us further of this were the Flemish painters working in the small church nearby. They, too, were directing their gaze at the sometimes sublime, sometimes terrifying book of nature. It didn't really matter, then, that our friend Stigliola, much like Bruno, spoke about an infinite universe of stars and animate planets while I argued that only a hateful God could have wished to amass stars and planets, devoid of fire, around this icy rock veined with blood. What really counted was that there did not exist any theory that we could not accommodate or dissect and in which disagreement and respect were not allowed the luxury of walking hand in hand. What ingenuousness we possessed! What an irony of fate! With much affection and hesitation do I then gather the messages of the Della Portas, of Pignatelli or of other friends of the Academy of the Svegliati, who assure me that I will soon be exonerated. I hope that they may not be wrong. But how many other unfounded accusations will I yet have to endure? How much enmity?

~ 3 ~

Michael

Saranac Lake, New York—May 2006

His mother had decided on the name, inspired by an old catalog of Michelangelo's David, which had been left in the house by his grandfather along with some other odds and ends. That his grandfather had died was part of the order of things; that he, Michael, was still alive was pure chance. Having been abandoned as a child by his father with no qualms, he had grown up like a cactus plant, kept alive by sporadic watering and plenty of natural light. He was thin, wiry, hairless, and even emaciated when he had to skip a meal or two. He knew that fleshier and naughtier girls were attracted to him, much the same way as men over fifty were. However, he never experienced enduring romantic or sexual passions, and in the rare moments of yielding to an erection, he stood alone, closing his eyes, and visualizing white and shapeless shadows. That morning he had woken up at dawn, realized that the milk had expired days ago, and that the cereal at the bottom of the box would barely fill a small cup of coffee. So he settled on eating the flakes one at a time, picking them out of the box, and while Lucius, the cat, sat in his lap, he absent-mindedly drafted a list of things to do. He wanted to repair his fixed-gear bike, pass by the florist, buy a Gallic rose to plant in the garden, cut his nails with small scissors to avoid the sliced effect of nail clippers. His mother constantly repeated, "Either you start to plan your future now or you'll end up like your father." And every time she made this pronouncement, what came to mind was the scene when his father, coming home after one of his benders, bent over him, his shirt open, his chest sweaty, his breath disgusting. He had just turned nine. Today, despite being convinced that he was nothing like his slacker of a father, Michael had to admit that his mother's fears were not baseless. He had finished high school with a decent average. He knew how to write better than most of his friends, but he had no desire whatsoever to study for competitive admission tests. Besides which, even though he was not an Olympic rower, he hoped he could join a rowing team and perhaps secure a scholarship to a college not too far from home. True, every now and then he did think about the universities in large cities, but he never managed to imagine a life far from his cat, far from the shores of the lake, or from the peace and quiet that they had found at home after his father left. Saint Luke University was a few minutes away. Maddie, a childhood friend of his, spoke about it enthusiastically every time she visited him. It seemed to be the easiest choice and, all things considered, the most reasonable. All of a sudden, he sprang out of his chair, and while Lucius rolled around on the ground, he undressed, gazed for a second in the mirror, felt pleased with his image from head to toe. Then, with a slightly foolish grin on his face, he headed toward the shower. From the other side of the house, his mother, who had just woken up, loudly called to him, "Michael, are you still here?" "Always, Mom . . . always," he answered, like Narcissus to his Echo. However, the words hovered like a dialogue between two deaf people.

He had kept his nose clean, so to speak, written the preparatory essays, and filled out any and every application form required of him. He had to do a short interview with an elderly administrator who began by singing the praises of Saint Luke University and upper New York State, about which Michael knew more than the administrator in question and the virtues of which he would have found hard to extol.

"It is truly a joy that a healthy and *simple* young man such as yourself has decided to register at Saint Luke . . . and obviously, I use the term 'simple' in the best sense of the word," decreed the administrator.

Michael thought he meant *poor*, but instead he answered like this: "Why go elsewhere when one of the best universities in the world is at your doorstep." Then, realizing that he sounded as if he were spouting nonsense but without wishing to veer too far from the banalities of the situation, he added, "Or at least one of the best for someone like me who prefers classes with a small number of students and professors dedicated to teaching."

"Clearly, since you live in the neighborhood, you know our university very well. But can you tell me if you have some idea of what you'd like to study here at Saint Luke?"

Michael was engulfed in a moment of confusion. Was it really necessary, he asked himself, to go beyond pleasantries?

So he improvised: "Well, I really couldn't say. I know that I like foreign languages, philosophy, the visual arts, but maybe I should try something completely new."

"Something you've never done before, to get out of your comfort zone, to break you out of your shell, so to speak," interrupted the administrator.

Hell, I've been reduced to a newborn chick! Michael silently observed, feeling both offended and amused, but he went on, giving his parting shot: "In other words, not only to get out of my comfort zone but to fly high, to fly towards new horizons." The old man gave a sly smile and continued in the same fashion. According to all standards of decency and mediocrity, the interview was a success. Indeed, the administrator had appreciated Michael's bashfulness and his eager attentiveness. He had been pleasantly surprised that a boy from this rather impoverished corner of America had responded with the candor and good manners of his more affluent peers. It felt good to believe in his mission of social equality, at least for a few hours. So Michael counted on being admitted, but since he was not absolutely certain and in order to pick up some extra cash, he found himself a summer job in a small organic grocery store.

Working at Nature's Store was by no means objectionable. In a place like Saranac Lake, it was almost the equivalent of a Cartier boutique with the added advantage that at the end of a shift, he was always able to bring a little something home to nibble on. He loved kosher yogurt, sunflower seeds (a recent discovery of his), and practically every variety of granola available in the store. After two months, there were faces he had learned to recognize as well as clients with whom he could happily chat. In short, he felt at home, and it was also for this reason that when Lara entered the store, he felt struck by a bolt of lightning on a clear day. When he started at Nature's Store, he didn't have great expectations: he would come into contact with the community and the merchants in the neighborhood, and maybe—he conjectured with a hint of sarcasm—he would make inroads into the hearts of the well-to-do female senior citizens of the area. Never would he have predicted that this job could lead to anything more. Lara's appearance in the store, however, was proving him wrong, or so he hoped. With her ash-blond ponytail, hazel eyes, and her cream-colored sweater (with the entire range of preppy colors of proper society), she turned to him with an amused and quizzical expression, as if she were facing a long-standing friend who was pretending not to know her. "Hi. How are you? Aren't you fed up with standing behind a cash register? What should we do?" And in just a few seconds, he felt as if he were succumbing to her. In any case, if it were some kind of comic skit that Lara wanted to enact, Michael would not have avoided going along with it. These were endless weeks. Lara always came into the store at different hours, and every time the bell rang, he gave a start. He would have liked to talk to her, ask her out for coffee, find out why she was in town, and why she sounded so sassy. However, he barely managed to smile at her. At first, Michael's smile radiated some measure of seductive appeal, but after several weeks, he wasn't able to elicit more than a baffling sense of antagonism from her. And so, it came to pass that Lara became more and more distant, more ethereal, progressively metamorphosing from a woman into a statue of salt. Nonetheless, since in the universe nothing stands still and everything changes, by the end of summer, Lara and Michael could think of themselves as good friends, "just friends," as they often had to clarify to the elderly clients' mischievous inquiries. In fact, it was actually as a friend that

Michael was able to discover that there were no secrets or mysterious reasons to cast a shadow on Lara's presence in Saranac Lake. She, too, just like him, would start university at the end of August. More precisely, her parents had bought her an apartment a few minutes from the campus, and Lara had decided to move there before the start of the term so as to begin decorating it. The rest of her family had stayed in Tupper Lake, a resort located on a bend in the Raquette River not far away—a fact that, together with the apartment purchased for their daughter in her twenties, indicated to Michael that he had very little in common with Lara. Despite this, as anyone working in an organic grocery knows well, and as Michael quickly learned, old money—namely, what is passed down from generation to generation—rarely is displayed with ostentation, or at least so it was in northern New York State, and so it was with Lara.

Saint Luke University, Saranac Lake,
New York—September 2006

Summer breezed by and left a slight scent of cotton candy in the air. After working uninterruptedly for three months, Michael was fully prepared to give up the role of adult. Nothing, then, could entice him more than sharpened pencils, phosphorescent highlighters, and all the social activities organized by the university for first-year students. He said to himself, "Now begins a new life, one that erases my father and my current life." He would reinvent himself. He would start over, maybe with another name, another body, another sex. He burst out laughing. What nonsense! He knew he would never change his name, that at most he would put on a pound or two, and as for his sex, which he proudly carried between his legs and adored, he would never do without it. He also had no doubts about one other thing: this entrée into Saint Luke University would be a watershed moment in his life. He would have to forget everything else and focus on important things: new pencils, multicolored highlighters, and an agenda to lose in the space of a few weeks.

In the hallway leading to all the classrooms, he chanced upon Lara, who seemed more reserved, more subdued, and tenser than usual. When she caught sight of him walking up the stairs, she smiled at him. It was more than a form of greeting, but it was not a real expression of joy. "So here you are. You didn't sneak off. You actually came!" she called out from afar. "Yes. Sorry to have disappointed you, madam. You'll have to share your desk with a pitiful sales clerk." But as soon as the words were out of his mouth, he regretted them. What was that about, calling her "madam"? Maybe Lara would think she had offended him. He was trying to be ironic so as to shake her out of melancholy. Obviously, he failed. So he tried again: "Okay, seriously, how are you? I've missed you in the store these last few weeks." A cloud passed over her face. By all accounts, he had made it worse.

"I'm fine!" said Lara. "It's my father who's having problems at work. I had to go back home to help my mother. All things considered, it's a good thing classes have started. It will help to distract me . . . and I will finally be able to see the legs of my favorite sales clerk! You can't see much of whoever stands behind the cash register."

Lara's face assumed an expression somewhere between mockery and malice. But in the meantime, Michael had regained his good humor. The morning's flattery about his legs was just what a great start to his first year in university should be. And just when he felt his enthusiasm was giving him a push into open water, he was assailed by the sad image of his mother, rejected and abandoned in her house along the river, relegated to a life of solitude. When all was said and done, what had she got out of raising a deserter only capable of loving in hindsight? Whereas his life was moving full speed ahead, hers was on the wane, she herself fading like an over-the-hill Ophelia, a willow battered by the currents, already far from eyes too ravenous for adventure to turn around and look backward.

The enthusiasm of these first days quickly gave way to a constant and distressing sense of fatigue. The courses were not particularly challenging, but there was always some new essay to write, some exam to prepare for. He slogged through his homework in the evening and practiced rowing at six in the morning. This routine ate into the few hours he allotted to sleep, and sleep itself became a kind of wormhole to crawl into. During the day, he walked around in a chronic state of insomnia, but he persisted because he felt a sense of fraternal exhilaration with the members of his sculling team because when they rowed together, it felt as if they were breathing in unison. For the first time in his life, he felt as if he belonged to something greater than himself, but he also began to wonder about the meaning of the word "family." In fact, even though only a few weeks had passed since the start of school, he could positively state that Jackson and Lucas, the captains of the rowing club, represented his family. They were in their last year, he, barely into his first, and yet, for some inexplicable reason, they seemed to be competing for his affection, encouraging him, constantly helping him, without ever burdening him. He was only sorry that he could not join them in the evening at the bar or at various parties where they were unfailingly treated as special guest stars. In reality, although Jackson and Lucas never committed indiscretions of any kind, he was convinced that those nights spent at various fraternity and sorority houses always ended on a high note. Tall, athletic, and perfectly matched— Jackson, the redhead, with wide shoulders, in other words, the fox, and Lucas, the agile, feline blond—he found himself imagining them semi-naked, their soccer shorts around their ankles, busy engaging in vigorous sexual acts. You had to be pretty blind not to notice how the girls gazed at them, and then again, they weren't to blame. Who could possibly resist Jackson's sculpted legs? Who could turn away from Lucas's pale grayish and innocent eyes? To know more about them, he would have to wait a year. At any rate, he told himself, his interest in them was probably nothing serious, nothing too complicated. As far as his own nights were concerned, he was forced to spend them with other first-year students and, when possible, at dinner with his mother, a mother who, from the moment Michael had left home, was aging before his very eyes. Resigned to this reclusive life, he was barely able to hide his surprise when, in the midst of talking about this and that, Jackson suggested they spend a weekend together in New York. The offer seemed harmless enough, but Michael's silence was immediately interpreted as hesitation by Jackson, who felt the need to add, "Come on, we'll have a great time," pronouncing these words in a kind of gruff, raspy voice. Fortunately for them both, the exchange ended there, but that automatic yet animal sound, which had escaped Jackson, terrified him. He stiffened, hastily accepted, and almost mechanically headed toward the dormitory in a state of neurotic euphoria.

New York, New York—December 2006

They had decided to leave at the end of the week of classes, and when they had fired up the Jeep Wrangler, it was just

4:00 P.M. He had haphazardly thrown his things into the trunk but made sure to place his shirts carefully so that they wouldn't wrinkle too much. For the trip, he had chosen his best underwear and doused himself with perfume. He had told himself that designer briefs and wafting mists of cologne must represent city life. Lucas and Jackson, on the other hand, latched on to a bottle of gin as soon as they climbed into the car but not in a frenzied fashion in the least: they had a lackadaisical way of doing things and behaved like older and rougher men than they really were. The curves the car took mimicked the zigzagging of their twisted and directionless souls, and anyway, that evening all roads would lead to New York. Destiny, thought Michael, is truly inescapable. It was almost eight when they arrived at the hotel, exhausted by the trip but also by the diverse expectations that each of them secretly nurtured within and, maybe even more, by their inability to articulate them. Lucas collapsed into an immediate and deep sleep. Jackson dove into the shower right away, and he, Michael, stretched out onto the bed beside Lucas with his pack of cigarettes squashed beneath his back. He was too tired to fall asleep, but he would try anyway to relax a bit. Removing his socks in this room with one bed and three men, in a hotel never before seen but that had seen everything, then placing his bare feet on the dirty carpet, he felt the absolute freedom of the moment, like a "go screw yourself" shout to the world, spoken without anger. All in all, this had to be real happiness.

Jackson came out of the shower, his towel wrapped tight around his waist. His hair looked molded to his head, and as usual, his forelock was perfectly in place. He had some hairy down on his chest and all around his navel. His Adam's apple protruded from his neck like a second nose. He smiled briefly at the sight of Lucas lying on the bed dead tired. He hung his wet towel on the chair and approached Michael to steal a cigarette from him. He lit it, said nothing, and began to smoke standing there completely naked except for the flip-flops on his feet. And then, without bothering to put on anything, headed toward the chair and dropped into it, leaving his legs carelessly spread apart. Michael tried not to look at his huge appendage, which hung there in the center of his body like some kind of fish, gasping for air and unaware that he would soon have to succumb to the fury or the whims of men. "Would you like to take a drag?" Jackson asked him after a while. Michael was uncertain whether he heard the question an hour or a minute later.

Lucas's eyes jerked open. By contrast, he got up very slowly and moved like a clumsy Siamese cat. A second earlier, he had been sound asleep. A second later, there he was, walking around like a blind man treading on his jeans and T-shirts, scattered here and there on the carpet. He stopped only after he extracted a cigarette from his pack, and then he headed straight for the shower in between one drag and another. Michael wondered if Jackson's and Lucas's gestures, seemingly spontaneous, did not belong to some kind of routine that—so he imagined—had been developed over the years by other weekends like this one, similarly enlivened by the gullible sucker of the moment. And yet he sensed a sort of cynicism, or at least a touch of mild indifference, in their lethargy. On campus, they had seemed to him to be two cheerful overgrown babies, always ready for new adventures and small acts of cruelty, whose ultimate goal was inevitably to get drunk. Here in New York, instead, they shed their skin like snakes. Perhaps they were more authentic, less stressed . . . difficult to say. At any rate, this unusual aloofness made him uncomfortable. He wasn't sure how to deal with it. It required learning a new language. Of course it was possible to blame it on the fatigue of the trip, the vulnerability felt by even the most intrepid of men, when taken out of his natural habitat. But there was something else: you could cut the air with a knife. Jackson felt it too because, as if to free himself from the tension, he pounced on the stereo in the corner of the room, inserted an old Coldplay CD, and took out a bottle of vodka he had hidden under the lining of his bag in case of a search by the highway patrol. Then, with a timid and slightly mischievous smile, he said, turning to Michael and Lucas, "What do you say? Shall we dance?" All of a sudden, Jackson and Lucas sprang to their feet with a bounce and, after standing still for a second, began to wiggle and twist their hips. Michael decided to join them. They were three idiots and a mirror, and when looking at the three of them framed by the mirror, he was reminded of the young musicians in a painting by Caravaggio that Leyla had shown him in one of her classes on Renaissance art.

They ended up in a club on Mott Street where Little Italy fades into the labyrinth of the borough of Nolita. Relaxed, brilliant, magnificent. That they would achieve success was a foregone conclusion. However, all they wanted was a night among friends and they had decided not to push it further. So they dropped the two unsuspecting and unfortunate girls they had ensnared at the club's exit and went back to the hotel with Michael, totally hammered, and clutching the remains of some cheeseburgers that they'd picked up when they had fallen prey to the munchies. After dragging themselves with difficulty through half-empty streets, they climbed the stairs two by two. They threw themselves onto the bed fully clothed, using their last bit of strength to kick their shoes and socks off, or as in the case of Lucas, not even. Michael took off his jeans and stretched out on the narrow strip of bed left free. When he woke up around nine in the morning, the others were still sleeping. During the night, Lucas had finally lost his socks, whether on purpose or by chance was difficult to say. Jackson, on the other hand, was only in his briefs, perhaps having been overcome by the heat. Michael wondered what the hell he was doing with them, who were so alike but so different from him. Why had they taken him along with them? What was he adding to their *twosome*? He thought, "For them, I represent the good deed of the month, the savage to be civilized." And yet, after wasting a half hour playing with his cell phone, he made up his mind that he couldn't care less about why and how. Whatever the motives spurring these two rich brats to bring him along, he was really happy to be in New York. The light entering the room had something urban about it—was that possible?—and was already springlike. From the window, he could see a small city park where men and women of all ages were flailing their arms about without much energy and even lesser spirit. Two mothers, whose deep dark circles under their eyes revealed their exhaustion, were chatting listlessly, and every now and then, they glanced over at their children who were cavorting madly around them. Wandering around the room, he noticed the latest issue of *New Age* beside the dresser. On the horoscope page, he read some advice for how to better confront the upcoming conjunction of stars: "Venus rising in Mars will amplify the attractiveness of those born in Virgo, predisposing them to risks and adventure." Michael was born on September 5. All he had to do was wait for Venus to enter the house of Cancer.

PART 2

Thomas Eakins, *Thomas Eakins and John Laurie Wallace on a Beach*, ca. 1883.

Caravaggio, *The Seven Works of Mercy*, 1607.

～ 4 ～

Michael

That first year of university cascaded around him like white-water rapids. At the beginning of the previous summer, Jackson and Lucas had moved on to the next phase in their predetermined lives, and once they had graduated, they vanished like cormorants at the first hint of an autumnal chill. Jackson had rented a room for himself and the girl whom he would marry six years later. Once exams were over, Lucas, too, had taken off for summer vacation. In short, these once-inseparable friends ended up being little more than long-standing acquaintances and, similar to trains at a standstill for too long, departed the station in opposite directions at matching speeds. Reflecting on the exchanges that characterized his relationship with Jackson before the latter's graduation, Michael felt that he had been stupid, that he had wasted time. Hoping that a relationship, which he himself had preferred to keep secret, could last longer than a season made him certainly guilty of naivete. Looking back, he was especially ashamed of the interminable bouts of hysteria that he had dumped on Jackson each and every time that discussions around cohabitation with "his" Martha had come up. Lucas, in the meantime, had drifted away, in part because he was excluded from the relationship between Michael and Jackson and in part because he had been plunged into a vortex of financial insecurity, which in turn had resulted in a distasteful obsession with money. What emerged from all this was that by the time the new school year had come around, literally nothing was left of their trio. All alone on campus (Lara, too, had left following an issue of fiscal fraud, which had engulfed her grandfather and father, and about which he knew next to nothing), Michael had no choice but to go back to square one. During his first year, hanging around Lucas and Jackson had offered him a framework in which to operate, a living space, as well as the security necessary to emerge from his cocoon of inexperience. Now, on his own, just the thought of peeking at the world outside and making new friends made him feel faint. Of course, he still sometimes indulged himself by recalling his adventures with Jackson before the advent of Martha, before unavoidable choices were made. Over and over again, he replayed in his imagination the scene of their first time together. It was an early summer night. Big talker Jackson was on a roll, and the two of them could not stop laughing. That evening, they had wandered aimlessly for hours, until seeing a small beach on the banks of the Saranac River. Jackson didn't hesitate for a second; using a well-practiced maneuver, he completely undressed and dove into the water, insisting that Michael join him. On other occasions, Michael would have balked or refused the invitation outright. But there was a new boldness in Jackson, a natural sense of initiative that emanated from each gesture of his, along with the beauty of the soft down on his sculpted chest (of which he was very proud) and his alabaster calves. Michael had already understood that his rapturous reactions to Jackson went beyond admiration. During that first intimate encounter, he gradually realized that resisting his new friend would not only have been useless but silly as well. While he was still hesitating about diving into the water, Jackson was already pulling and pushing him toward the shore, with the ability to flip him like the page of a book. He was everywhere—above him, inside him. And inside him, that night had never ended because every spasm and shudder had shown the force of an awakening, even if afterward, months away from that beach, the experience seemed shrouded in a hazy mist. Meanwhile, the days had turned monotonous again, a long drawn-out necklace of pearls without beginning or end. It was better for him to devote himself to his studies, to the short thesis that Leyla, his art history professor, had asked him to finish as quickly as possible and, "if you do not mind," bring directly to her home.

Leyla's house was only a few steps from the campus, but once he arrived at the entrance to the cottage, it seemed to Michael as if he had been wandering around for hours. He had listlessly dragged himself from the library to the address Leyla had written on a piece of paper. He had nothing on his agenda for the rest of the day and had calculated that if he allowed himself a little longer to get there, he wouldn't have to wrack his brain to find something to do in those sure to be miserable hours following this meeting. As he walked, he kicked the pebbles on the path, discovering now and then tiny shoots of green buried under the dust. The dust, in fact, prevented the emerging weeds from making headway by keeping them flattened down. It seemed cruel. He felt an immense pity for that unwanted bit of nature and for himself because of the state of neglect and indifference into which he had sunk of late. Since Lucas and Jackson had left, the days seemed interminable, his energy level had dropped to zero, and he painfully reflected that if Jackson and Lucas had been around, he wouldn't be passing the time futilely rearranging stones. But even this subtle anger did nothing more than produce a slight kick from him, which in turn produced a slight cloud of dust. From afar, he probably looked like a child cheerfully releasing his energy on a ball of paper. But in reality, he felt about as energetic as a rag doll. It was already dark when he reached Leyla's front door. Dusk had traced a red streak in the sky, and above it, there was a threatening curtain of cloud. Here on the ground among mortals, the fog was thicker than usual. He nervously rang the bell with the insistence of someone who wants to get it over with.

As he rang the bell, he realized that the front door was completely ajar, and once inside, he had the strange sensation that a post-apocalyptic scene might have been orchestrated a few minutes before his arrival in an effort to send a "please help me" message. Leyla's house was in a state of chaos—open boxes on the floor, not entirely emptied—remnants of an incomplete move. Books of every type and size lay on tables among the dirty breakfast dishes. And where was Leyla in all this? Had she rushed all of a sudden to the university, to a meeting she had forgotten about? Was she hiding in a semi-undressed state in hopes of being sought after? Maybe she had just gone to the bathroom for a second. These various scenarios were running through his mind when Leyla appeared at the top of the staircase like some deus ex machina. And then, there she was, teetering down the stairs on tiptoes because of her pregnant belly, all the while apologizing for the mess, for being late, and for every single object out of place that she spied as she descended the stairs. Upon seeing her like that, Michael, who was never very good at making small talk, smiled nervously. If he could have, he would have liked to leave his essay on the table and run away, but he was afraid that Leyla might chase him outside and devour him in one bite. In the meantime, she had sat down at a small table, moved a pile of books toward a corner, and after having pulled over a chair, signaled to Michael to approach. She then began to speak about the Madonna in *The Seven Works of Mercy*, the theme that she had instructed Michael to write about. She asked him how many other examples of the Madonna of Mercy he had come across in Neapolitan painting, if he had found any treatise dealing with the history of religions that could provide some elucidation on the function of the Madonna in Caravaggio's painting. And so Michael began to formulate an answer when a new and unexpected figure appeared at the top of the stairs like some figment of his imagination. "It's as if we are on stage," thought Michael, much amused. In fact, Pablo did sway a little self-consciously up there, and when he finally headed downstairs, he tried to do it as surreptitiously as possible. At any rate, each of his steps unleashed a kind of vibration that shook Michael to his very core, sending a rush of blood that, once pumped out of the heart, was detonated directly within his skull. For a brief moment, Michael feared that his ears would explode. Pablo likely realized this, too, because he decided to reverse his planned course of action and introduce himself to Michael.

During the course of Pablo's performance, Leyla squirmed in anger, conscious of having lost Michael's attention and all residual professional credibility. All of a sudden, she exploded, "Pablo, we're working! Take what you need and go." With that outburst, Michael understood from where the SOS signal was coming when he had entered the house. He would have liked to jump up, become a human shield to protect Pablo, take him aside, and tell him that all would be resolved, that he was not to blame, and that—contrary to what he might have come to believe—he, too, had the right to be loved. And precisely when these feelings were unconsciously emerging, Michael intuited but less clearly that mutual love does not exist, that one loves or is loved, and that the role of beloved object is often the more difficult one in that it requires decency, discretion, and a large dose of compassion. In the meantime, Leyla had regained control of the situation and of herself. At this point, it was a fight to the bitter end for her. "Here!" she said, turning to Michael, placing two books by the philosopher Tommaso Campanella in his hands: *The City of the Sun* and *Atheism Conquered*. "They're translated, with the original version on the opposite page. They should give you a bit of context. At any rate, they're two extremely rare books that I have been carrying around for years and that I've never lent anyone. I'm giving them to you because you deserve them."

A Month Later

By now, Pablo had become an obsession. It wasn't just his physical appearance or Michael's confused feelings for this perfect stranger but the distinct premonition that something serious and terrible was about to happen to him. It was perhaps because of this that, when he saw him at the top of Leyla's staircase, Michael mistook for love that which he now believed was an unusual vocation, a calling from above. Upon reading the books of Tommaso Campanella, lent to him by Leyla, he wondered if sexual appetite could propel the quest for the absolute in someone who did not believe in God. In fact, if he had to describe what he felt in relation to Pablo, he would need to employ the categorical imperative or other abstract terms of philosophical thought. It was a sense of responsibility, similar to the one that might make a person decide to take a dog home upon finding it badly beaten up at the side of a road, because ignoring it and moving on would mean condemning it to certain death. But what made Pablo's case more complicated were three things. Michael had listed them in an arithmetic exercise book, and this is how he summarized them: In the first place, Pablo was about to become a father—something that, together with his somewhat macho self-centeredness, would make him dote on Leyla. Two, not feeling himself to be in any danger—and why would he?—Pablo demonstrated a willful impudence. Last but not least, and this was what really bothered Michael, he and Pablo barely knew each other. Unfortunately, although he wracked his brains trying to come up with a strategy to see him more often, Michael could not concoct anything concrete. There was the difference in age, the fact that Pablo did not hang out in student circles, and all in all, there was the fact that although they belonged to adjoining worlds, these worlds were separated into sealed compartments. And so he launched himself on desperate ventures to "accidentally" bump into Pablo in order to hit on him. He passed hours and hours in the park in front of Leyla's house in hopes of being able to speak to him, sitting there distractedly and reading until sundown. He got himself assigned extra research work by Leyla in the rather pathetic hope of being reinvited into her house. But nothing had really worked. In quite a tragicomic way, the only thing that he had gained from all this was a series of academic conversations with Leyla and a vast knowledge of the intellectual circles of an early seventeenth-century Naples, from Campanella to Caravaggio, through Bruno, Della Porta, and others. He was feeling devastated and defeated. He was learning that true solitude was an absence of solutions, the dust in the air that one observed from a sofa while idly awaiting a call that would never come. He was distracted in school, distant from everyone. When he found the strength to work out, it was a way to waste time and use up the last bit of energy that he had to dispense. However, it was on one of these sporadic visits to the gym that he saw him again. Motivated more by pride than desire, he approached Pablo and began to speak to him. Surprisingly, Pablo appeared to be warm and friendly. In fact, dispelling any apprehension on the part of Michael, he readily engaged him in conversation, did not cut their interaction short— quite the opposite. They spent around ten minutes in which they discussed all kinds of things and in which Pablo did not abstain from asking questions, without exhibiting any ulterior motives and intentions. Michael concluded, "There is something unfathomable about this man." He then saw him in the locker room, naked like the Tahitians of Gauguin. He was a man without malice, without reservations, and without a modicum of physical modesty.

They met at the Cloakroom Lounge, one of the only, if not *the* only, cocktail bar in Saranac Lake serving pretty good cocktails despite its sordid atmosphere, its flaking floral wallpaper, and the creaky floor. As soon as Pablo entered, he burst out, "Sorry for being late! Leyla wanted me to help her put the crib together. She's terribly anxious about the baby coming, and it would have been impossible for her to assemble the pieces by herself." Michael listened good-naturedly, coming to the conclusion that Pablo must be the type of man who always has a ready but perfectly reasonable excuse. "No worries!" he said. "It's not as if I had that much to do." He was already capitulating, or maybe he was just trying, not without some hostility, to highlight the difference between himself and Leyla.

"So how are you doing?"

"Me? How am *I* doing?" responded Pablo with a smile. "Um, that's not a question that is often put to me. Let's see. . . . I'm tired, anxious, content. Considering the circumstances, I'm okay." So Michael took a chance on a verbal jab, "For circumstances, you mean the person hemming you in?" He immediately regretted it. It was an exaggeration. He had gone too far. But he didn't even have the time to rectify the situation because Pablo had an instantaneous answer: "I wish she hemmed me in a little more! If only she needed my help. Leyla keeps me at arm's length." Michael smiled. An obscenity came to mind, something that had to do with getting one's hands on him.

And as if to intercept this thought, Pablo whispered, "I'm of Peruvian origin. Physicality is important to me. Maybe I'm a stereotypical male, but I'm a stereotype that likes to get laid." In that moment, both of them conspicuously swallowed the saliva that welled up in their mouths. The conversation had all of a sudden taken a salacious turn, and it had become clear to both of them what they were driving at, in that dive bar, a few minutes before one in the morning. Pablo pulled his stool closer to Michael's, promptly leaned toward his girlfriend's student, and spoke in a low voice. "Can I whisper something in your ear?"

It had been weeks since he had visited his mother and he was taken aback by the shambles the house was in and by the similarity between her house and Leyla's. It perplexed him. Did this mean that this was the destiny of every woman who was alone: a progressive emotional deterioration, the loss of the preservation instinct? Even worse, he wondered if these were the first signs of some form of senile dementia. He still had the keys and so he had automatically opened the door without knocking. For a brief moment, he feared that he would find his mother stretched out on the floor, dead for days, having been attacked by some drug addict or by thieves who had broken into the house. Then he saw her, busy shuffling boxes around, completely unaware that another human being, and a man no less, was in her house. He didn't reveal his presence right away. Instead, he observed her from afar, like a ghost would, or someone who, once they have lost a beloved person, imagines her still there in the usual places. Like a wraith, his mother appeared younger, more ethereal, despite her gray hair, her worn-out slippers, and the wool housecoat she had been wearing for years. It shamed him to think that had he been a different man, that dressing gown could have been easily removed and he could have taken her from behind. On the other hand, it had been more or less this way with all the men in her life, his father included. "I'm unworthy. I deserve nothing," his mother continuously repeated in a refrain that had marked the rhythm of their lives. Today, instead, she was humming. And it was that sound, imitated and then superseded by the song of a sparrow hawk in the garden, that jolted him out of the torpor into which he had sunk the moment he had crossed the threshold. It was a spell that shattered like a glass bowl. He called to her once, twice, "Mom . . . Mom."

She turned around, squinted, and exclaimed effusively, "Oh! Here you are," almost as if she had lost him among her boxes and finally found him again. In her gaze and in the fullness of her smile, there was no sign of rancor, no trace of sadness but the unhoped-for joy of having her son restored to her, of having him materialize by rummaging through old photos. She then explained to Michael that she had been spending days trying to reorganize the photographs. She took him by the hand to show him and guide him through a photo album that was obviously devoted to him, Michael, and in which she, his mother, was either absent, off to the side, or often cut in half. He saw himself at two years of age, in mittens and a wool hat, which for some unknown reason had been seared into his memory. Here he was on his first day of school, with his brand-new uniform just out of its plastic packaging. And here he was at his seventh birthday party, one to which his father, inspired by some sudden sense of purpose, showed up at a time when he was employed by a used car dealership and from which he would be fired a few days after the party. In the first photo of that unforgettable birthday, his father appeared way off to the side of the image and obscured to some extent by his mother. Despite this, a sense of foreboding engulfed Michael: he anticipated that this man, whom he had despised so much, would appear in the foreground of the photos in the album, forcing his mother into the background, into her usual position of subordination, of second best. He wasn't mistaken. His father was indeed there: with his acid-washed jeans, white T-shirt, leather vest, and his proud and dazzling smile. Michael appeared at the lower edge of the same photo, tiny next to his father and therefore, from his father's vantage point, invisible. He recognized the mustache that Michael had associated with a later period, when contact between them had become rarer. It surprised him to discover that the mustache had already existed in that earlier time. He scrutinized the face of this man who belonged in another life, and then he shifted his focus onto himself as a child: a Michael about whom he remembered little and whom he tried to recognize and commiserate with. He then explored again his father's face and the details framed between the stool where he was sitting and the man's mustache, and he suddenly understood. Deaf to the murmuring of his mother, who, from the moment he had begun to leaf through the album, had not stopped talking for a second, Michael began to feel shaky and unsteady. That stupid grin, that cocky mustache made of his father the spitting image of Pablo.

Lying next to him, Pablo slept the sleep of the just ("or that of fools," he thought, giggling to himself), while he, having just awakened, minutely examined him from head to toe, lingering on the locks of hair that covered his face, the lines just noticeable on the sides of his mouth, the archipelago of moles between his shoulder and neck. Raising himself slightly and leaning against the headboard, he decided to stay in this position and read *The City of the Sun*, lent to him by Leyla, but also another book about Campanella, which he had miraculously found in the library (a kind of intellectual biography written by a Milanese scholar). Every now and then, however, he found it fun to spy on Pablo, to review every part of his body. "He is objectively beautiful," he said to himself. "I mustn't wake him." And while he was thinking this, Pablo's cell phone began to ring. Michael caught a glimpse of Leyla's name on the screen. All at once, he felt naked, a criminal caught in flagrante delicto. He hoped that Pablo would wake up and answer it quickly so that he could avoid the distress that the name on the screen was causing him. But Pablo was not giving any sign of life, lost as he was in a deep sleep. So he began to shake him lightly, with the indifference that an old lady would show in attempting to wake up her sleepyhead husband. Grimacing, Pablo grabbed the phone that had already stopped ringing. He scanned the name in the missed calls log and, once found, turned toward Michael with a glance both troubled and questioning. "It's Leyla," he exclaimed. As he waited for some sign of consent, he froze, a wind-up teddy bear in need of being recharged. So Michael spoke the magic words: "Call her. Call her right away." He pronounced them, hating himself in that instant, but he didn't feel that he had a choice since it was what the circumstances, the awful game they had been forced to play, demanded. Over the course of the telephone conversation, Pablo did not speak a word, uncommonly attentive, meticulously absorbing and breaking down the avalanche of information that was being unloaded onto him. Michael discovered, with a touch of pride, that Pablo was capable of concentration. In fact, he asked himself where had that other Pablo gone, the one who argued in circles about everything and nothing, without listening to even a word being said to him. Finally, he put the phone down onto the night table and straightened up like a tree trunk. "Leyla says she needs me. She had abdominal cramps last night and would like me to stay and sleep with her from now on." Michael would have liked to come up with some witty gibe, but in that moment, any response other than a nod of approval would have sounded out of place. He saw Pablo put on the pants and T-shirt he had been wearing the night before and decided that in the absence of any alternative plan of action, he would accompany him. In the car, Pablo didn't speak. It seemed he was making an effort to sort himself out, organizing the thoughts that crowded his mind. Michael stared at the road before them and waited for a sign. Once they reached the parking spot, Pablo turned to him with tears in his eyes and the grin of a satyr. "It's amazing. I'm going to be a father soon. Can you believe it? A father!" He uttered this, his voice filled with emotion. And what became obvious was something that Michael had suspected for a long time: Pablo was not his, nor had Jackson been his, nor would anyone ever be his. But while pondering the depth of his disillusionment, he recalled that he had left the Campanella books on the night table. He felt a burning sensation in his stomach: as usual, he had put others before himself and now he absolutely needed those books. In the last few weeks, he had decided to search for an answer to the mystery of Caravaggio's Neapolitan work among Campanella's circle of friends. When Leyla had called, he was in the midst of reading about a sex scandal involving Campanella among the Augustinians of Padua. He would have liked to know how that story ended, but to do that, he would have to go back home on foot. He felt utterly downcast and despondent. A solution for his mood existed: he could be consoled by retrieving those books and retracing the footsteps of Campanella. In doing so, he would escape into baroque Naples, which, whether through the fault or the merit of Leyla, had already thrown his life into disarray.

～ 5 ～

Tommaso Campanella

Padua, Republic of Venice—November 1593

When my imprisonment in Rome was over, I went back to Naples, hoping to devote myself to research and teaching. Yet once there, I had to surrender to a self-evident truth: scientific thought and the pursuit of freedom might never take root in such primitive minds. Besides, as the sequence of events that brought me here to Padua hath shown, I myself risk losing my life. But really, where could I go? To Cardinal Del Monte in Rome? To Grand Duke Ferdinand in Florence? When I decided to leave Naples, the final destination was not that important. I just hoped that I wouldn't sink again into the vortex of ignorance and prejudice that was closing in around me. I needed to breathe fresh air, bask in a ray of hope. Neapolitans, totally dedicated as they are to a life of shallow idiocy, have revealed themselves to be egocentric, haughty, and often vindictive. I gave up trying to advise them against the error of their ways because to attempt to conquer hostile and impoverished souls is a futile endeavor. But once I left Naples, I had to conclude that even outside the borders of the kingdom, what thou get from a courtier is nothing but fawning and flattery. No one listened to me in Rome or in Florence. No one heard my protestations. No one was ready to offer me protection or enduring support. In certain moments, I felt as if I were losing my mind. In Rome, for example, the cardinal glossed over everything as soon as the conversation turned to thorny issues. Instead, chattering on about everything and nothing, as we walked through damasked halls at the pace of marathon runners—the cardinal had healthy lungs!—he brought me to the music room of his palace, where the opulence of the paintings was replaced, with less splendor, by a sensuous performance by three young musicians playing lutes, viols, and cornets. My sojourn in Florence was not too different. There, I was insulted by the beneficence of the grand duke, but at least I had the opportunity to visit the Medici library—a wonder of the world. Again, no one listened. And yet, I am convinced that both Cardinal Del Monte and Grand Duke Ferdinand have read Telesius more than once, and that, ravenous and parched, they have quenched their thirst at the fountain of his words, like those who have lived in a desert of ignorance. Be that as it may, they are cowards as they are governed by the dominant discourse. And so they decided to cast aside the truth because this truth of Telesius is an uncomfortable out-of-date truth. They say that the times are not propitious, that the Holy Father would not approve. They do not add anything else. What to do, then? Shut my ears and mouth? Live in a dark rabbit hole? The grand duke hath confessed to me in secret that giving me a court appointment would be too risky. A rejection following on the heels of that of Cardinal Del Monte—with his gaze fixed on his corpulent boys, a hint of drool around his mouth—a rejection that pushed me farther north. Today, I find myself, almost by chance, at the monastery of the Augustinian friars in Padua, weary, heartsick, and deprived of the privacy that my state of health calls for. I share a cot with Brother Berardo, fortunately the kindest, handsomest, and most accommodating of the entire group. All my companions seem docile, but like sheep, they scrutinize me, sniff around me. Shall the night transform the sheep into wolves?

When my eyelids dropped down over my eyes like the north gate, I reawakened in the century of my new existence but this time with no hindrance to my prophetic consciousness. Not one of my previous dreams had ever been so revealing, and for the first time, I perceived the Mayan face of the father, whose voice, in earlier hypnotic evocations, I had not heard before. Strangely, I recognized him without hesitation. In this moment, however, the dream was interrupted, and in a kind of leap, I was carried far from that image and to a new stage that I was seeing from above, as when the moon turns toward the earth. Here, the Mayan father was talking to a bronzed and magnificent youth who called him Pablo (thus I discovered the Hispanic name of the sire), but the light was too feeble to allow me to distinguish words or movements. All of a sudden, I witnessed the father approach the angel and cover him proudly, as if to shake him. Then a slow struggle started between them, a real brawl, which quickly was revealed to be a ritual not too different from the mating of horses. But while the two of them were grasping at each other, I myself, being jolted in my sleep by others, felt that I was being plunged back into my present. At the same time, due to a certain physical resistance to waking up, I found myself inside another scene, another brief prophetic dream, which being closer to me in time and space—and the blue canopy confirmed it—must have corresponded to an immediate future, if not to the unfolding of my destiny. Now the eye of the dream fluttered over Roman roofs. Then, captivated by the draft passing through one roof, it penetrated it, following a ray of light, and finally spilled into an establishment with meagre and dusty furnishings. In the actual center of the large room, a flat mirror drove the ray of light toward a shield. From there, the same light projected and stamped the image of a dying eel onto a lead-white canvas. It was only after a few seconds, however, that the eye, accustomed to the peripheral obscurity of the room, became aware of another presence: two men slumped over on a straw pallet, sleeping the damp and heavy sleep that follows intemperance. Upon looking more closely, I had the immediate impression of recognizing who, between the two, was the painter of the canvas in the center, while I also wholly understood the feeble complacency of his younger errand boy. Thus I waited for them to wake up, and eavesdropping on their whispers, I was convinced about the painter's identity: it was Michelangelo da Caravaggio about whom so much hath been spoken by Manso's emissaries. It is as yet impossible for me to establish if my comprehension was determined by words, gestures, or by the interpenetration of the consciousnesses of others, all of which is characteristic of the dream. Nevertheless, I could sense that the two of them were set on abandoning their Roman dwelling and the few friends still left to them, that they were heading for the Spanish kingdom of Naples. This was an unshakable intuition, which the wounds and the bloodstains on the painter only confirmed. At this point, however, a sensation of both ecstasy and heartache took hold of my spirit. It was as if a carriage pulled by galloping horses crushed me with all the weight of the evidence, as if a prior future and an innocuous one, up until that moment, had already evolved and not without contradictions and impediments into an imminent near future.

Three Days Later

I left Naples, hoping for a better outcome. Alas, I find myself in this hole, the lowest point to which I have ever fallen, pursued by humiliating and incomprehensible accusations. The inquisitors have come here to the monastery of the Augustinians and are asking me for a summary of what happened the night before. They are relentlessly interrogating me to clarify the course of events. But how do I respond to defamatory insinuations when the nature of my involvement escapes even me? In fact, my memories lead back to the first hours of dinner. I recall, for example, the slightly bitter flavor of the goose sausage, the gnocchi of breadcrumbs, and a most fragrant rice enhanced by morsels of quail. I remember as well the full-bodied tannic wine offered to us by Ippolito Maria, the Augustinian master. Then everything becomes obscure and confused. Enormous segments of the evening remain dreamlike and shielded from my consciousness, as if the events slipped away, leaving no trace. The fact is that in the dining room, it was pitch dark, and with my vision damaged by the intensity of my studies, I did not see what was happening or perchance the real images could not be etched in my mind. They are accusing me now—and just the fact of recounting this fills me with horror—of having sodomized

Ippolito, of having been urged on by others, and of taking pleasure from doing this. And in spite of the necessity to defend myself against whoever tarnishes my name, I am nonetheless agonizing over the idea that there is no smoke without fire, that something must have happened. When I reflect again on my conduct in the last few months, I cannot exclude the possibility that a part of me hath been overwhelmed by this torpid adventure. There is still so little that I know about myself as well as so much that I suffer for myself, for Ippolito, for all of us. Nicola saith over and over again that the wine and sausage had been drugged, that we were all framed. For my part, I wonder if there exists a fly that doth not secretly yearn for the spider's web. Some time ago, Della Porta said to me that a look alone can corrupt the most pious of men, but I ask myself if that look may not be the rope to which our soul clings to wade across the narrow stream that separates good from evil. O that God may enlighten me! May He have mercy on me! And may the stars guide Tommaso Campanella!

Around Three Months Later

I was cleared of the accusations of the Augustinians, no one doth know whether by luck or the slothfulness of the inquisitors, and having inscribed myself at the University of Padua, I came into contact with astrologers of international repute and surrendered myself to the theories of Della Porta. To be precise, more than "surrendered." I should say that having acquired concrete proof of his theories, it did not seem as if I had any other choice. How else otherwise could I have understood the unfortunate story of the German Valentin Nabod without resorting to astrology? How could I have interpreted my own destiny? It was to Padua where, since reading about imminent perils in the stars, Nabod ran for cover, segregating himself in the house and locking doors and windows. But since it was impossible to tamper with fate, it was in that house that he met his death, butchered by thieves whom he had believed he could escape. In my case as well, the astral conjunction that hath allowed me to confer with the most brilliant minds of our century cannot be purely coincidental. However, it's pointless to deny, even here in Padua, I encountered backward, small-minded, arrogant beings. And if in most cases I let it go—whether it be out of fatigue or the desire for a quiet life—I felt an obligation to intervene when the attacks on my friends became more pernicious. The question is this: "How can we still affirm in the style of Galen of Pergamon that there is a spirit in the liver, another in the brain, and a third in the heart? It becomes inevitable to ask if for them, these Aristotelian zealots, there are no spirits in our flatulent wind?" In defense, in the name of my friends, like Persio, employing all good sense, I threw myself into the philosophical battlefield, arguing that if spirit exists, it is none other than a puff of air that permeates and vitalizes everything, starting in the brain and radiating through our limbs, so as to shepherd them like a puppet its strings. Indeed, if there ever were a question, I would be intrigued to know what happens to this spirit of ours once the body ceases to be. Will it travel across time and space? Will it transmigrate into the body of an Amerindian four hundred years into the future like my dream seems to indicate? Or will it reunite with the body in the earth and, decomposing as the body doth, become new fodder?

Having been arrested in the middle of the night, this is to be my third trial. I was with Ottavio Longo when it happened. As usual, we were playing cards until the first light of dawn, cheating once in a while in order that fun might have the better of sleep, talking, not without some sense of melancholy, about our far-off villages, and about seasons long past. In particular, having recounted tales of the Calabrian countryside and my childhood spent in the hedgerows chasing butterflies or plucking the bright yellow flowers from the broom trees, I was about to describe the pale complexion of my mother when, interrupted by the guards, I was torn from my friends. The accusation? That of composing blasphemous sonnets, debating with Jews, possessing manuals dealing with geomancy, and who knows what else. About geomancy, I must admit, they didn't state anything false, also because there is no text that they haven't added to the index of prohibited books, even though reading and consulting about it might not have bothered anyone until yesterday. As for the sonnets, I did not understand what they referred to; to be honest, I couldn't say what was blasphemous in their mind. I only know that in this round of investigations, the inquisitors appear to be much fiercer, deafer, and more pitiless, and the closer we get to the end of the century, the steeper the incline we have to reascend. Never before as in this trial did they persecute me so much. Never have they shown so much sadism and cruel indifference in their lust for torturing me. I hope, then, that the escape orchestrated by Nicolò, Francesco, and Isaac doth not end up costing us our skin, but it is certain that the transfer from Venice to the cells of Sant'Angelo doth not augur well. I console myself, however, and at the same time, I am disheartened by the fact that they have not spared anyone, that they have caught us all: the most eminent voices of a century, those who for me represented great teachers. It is said, in fact, that Stigliola, Bruno, and Filidino are prisoners here as well, reduced to names without faces, they, too, victims of the Roman

Inquisition. Together, we are living in the nostalgic and horrible expectation of the end—that stretching out upon the world's ultimate pyre. And as every heavy thing is directed toward the center of the earth and just as the faint-hearted and jocund weasel runs into the mouth of the monster who then will devour it, so, too, whoever hath ventured onto the open seas of knowledge at the call of Ulysses will find himself with me in this pitiful hospice. I would like to call this place of weeping and sighing the cave of Polyphemus, the palace of Atlantis, the labyrinth of Crete, and yet it is without vacillation of any kind that I must—that I will not hesitate—to call it the mouth of hell.

Three Years Later

I do not wish to die. Today for the first time, as every strip of my body is mutilated by my jailers, while every single joint of mine feebly cracks like the shell of an egg, today more than ever, I have understood that I cherish this withered skin of mine and these few and mangled bones, that I cherish them even more than my soul.

Liberation and Exile, Kingdom of Naples—July 1598

Condemned to exile, I was sent back to Calabria and thus thrown once more into the belly of enemy territory from which, with so much suffering, I had once succeeded in extricating myself. Have no fear, it will be from there that I must start over! For he who hath the thick skin of a pachyderm, in fact, it is never too late to invent another destiny for himself, a new date of birth, even when being reborn means dying a little. And so now in my native land, I place myself at the head of a revolution that will put history back on its rightful path.

I will do this thanks to the support of Ponzio and Pinzoni. I will do it for all those who in Naples, as here in this country-side, have had to pay the excise duty of Spanish criminals. Let them think that they have annihilated me because our vendetta will be more terrible and their fates so much more ominous when the axe of the Most High will fall on them. Of course, it is not worth denying it: rarely, in life have I known a humiliation similar to that of returning to the ancestral home, my tail between my legs. But it was a necessary humiliation. We had been mistaken to think we could subvert the world order while leaving behind those for whom we were fighting. We were operating from afar, and the winds of revolt would have had to blow more fiercely to carry its seeds to such arid lands. Now it is necessary to play for time, pound the earth day after day, make the benefits of water understood, and bathe the earth with fresh new water. Since that wretched day when I was brought back to Calabria, I awaken at dawn and, armed with courage and infinite patience, I go with Ponzio and Pintoni to knock on doors. On the happier days, we are welcomed with a smile and a bowl of goat's milk, but we do not stop even when the doors remain closed or one's knuckles burn from the cold. Our hearts are filled with the hope of a doctrine that can defeat fear and cure ignorance. "What are you telling us?" they ask us. "What instruments can we make use of?" Truth and love are our music, our instrument. We are educating these poor brothers of ours. We explain to them the iniquities of the Spanish yoke. Then in moments of discomfort, we reveal to them the message of the stars, which ignite these Calabrian skies on chilly winter nights, and tracing an astral alphabet with a finger, we pinpoint the smile of God. Because the outcome is of little importance to us: even when it's hard to see it, a man struggling for his dignity is already a free man.

I understand only now, in the hour that follows the final surrender, that there are no ropes and chains that encircle with a more sensuous hold, insults that grip the stomach with forceps more violent than betrayal itself. Compared to that, torture is like a caress, the piss of the guards—which hath already splashed my face—holy water poured on me. We needed a few weeks so that the revolution planned in the early days of summer would deliver the desired effect. Without ever taking a break and being ferocious like a winter storm, I managed to convince our more hesitant companions, also thanks to the help of Dionisio Ponzio. Our blessed Father Clement supported us with caution, following our movements from Rome, without compromising himself. As a consequence, in the hours when our knees were creaking and our calves seemed chained to the ground, knowing that the Holy Father was on our side infused our hearts with courage and gave us new impetus in our undertaking. When we began our campaign of conversion and recruitment, we were four brave friends. After a year, we would have difficulty counting the comrades and followers. Never over the course of the long months did we ever lose heart, even when the destination seemed unreachable, even where our ideas clashed with the practical exigencies of men and women who had no resources or time. Encouraged by starry prophecies and the strength of our bond, we often discovered premonitions of change in the sky and in the book of the world. But what really convinced us that the wind was blowing in our favor were the hundreds of peasants and laborers, men and women, who, laying down pail and shovel, followed us to the death. From whom then could the volte-face have emanated if not from two solitary and feeble wolves already alienated

from the pack, two outlaws without skill or talent and therefore untried in the nature of faith? Fabio di Lauro and Gio-
van Battista Biblia: they were the henchmen of the devil, the
snakes attached to the Virgin's breast, tenants of the most
colossal cesspit. They were the ones who betrayed us. A
painstakingly built house of cards was thus set to collapse,
and in the dusty aftermath of the crash, our glorious Calabrian revolution ended. And to say that we would have
wanted to reunite the destitute of the Mediterranean, that
we had already lined up about sixty ships on the Turkish
coastline! We could have vanquished the opposition of all the
parish priests and local squires sheltering under the Spanish
mantle. But then—when thinking about it—is it not the cor-
ruption and the callousness of our priests and lords that rob
this land of a future? On whom can we place the blame, then,
if not on ourselves, on the incorrigible ingenuousness of
Tommaso Campanella who could not see how a flash in the
night was enough to trigger the Count of Lemos and his
lackeys? Made more astute by the passing of the years and
with the refined ear of the she-wolf, the newly elected vice-
roy is all too aware of how little fire is needed to burn his
ruined lands. And so, like thieves in the night, we are fleeing the hounds unleashed by the count, sensing their breath
on our necks, their bloodthirsty wheezing, as they attempt
to flush us out. May Tommaso Campanella be cursed, he
who hath disappointed the stars, God, and his flock. And
may the seven bumps on his head also be cursed, for they are
the symbol and eternal reminder of shameful vanity.

A Little More than a Year Later

Ponzio and I were thrown out of an earthly paradise where
we had lived too short a time, like the nude and shameful

progenitors painted by Masaccio. They couldn't kill us solely based on the crimes committed by us. How else could they have justified it to our so widespread and fervent following? Alas, what they were doing was sharpening their wits, and thus, to the accusation of revolution they added the classic transgression of heresy.

We were loaded on a galley heading for Naples. There must have been around two hundred of us packed on board like dirty rags and, as such, trusting that we would pass unobserved. Four men hanged on the prow of the ship had, from the departure, accentuated every second that separated us from the wharf with their macabre swinging to and fro. In front of them and along the horizon line formed by the coast, we began, however, to distinguish a shapeless magmatic anthill. In fact, informed of our arrival, the Neapolitans were taking their leave of families and businesses, and having rushed toward the port, they thronged onto the quays of the waterfront by the thousands. Looking at them from the ship, they appeared to us as if they were stacked like straw, enthusiastic and rowdy like during the days of the Cockaigne pole. When we finally neared the port, we espied their voracious grins in more distinct detail; we heard their roar and, as we got closer, the bestial gnashing of their teeth. And although on the ship we stood one against the other, to protect ourselves from similar barbarities and to avoid what was awaiting us on shore, here was another spectacle of horror offered up to our eyes. With a sudden turn that flung us toward the stern, we were flanked by a second galley, this one also crammed with prisoners. A little farther off, we saw two more, similarly lined up. Within a few seconds, our sinister foreboding was overtaken by a more dreadful reality. Rifling through us as if we were a basket of clothing, the jailers removed two prisoners from the crowd. They pushed them to the ground and held them there by the scruff of their necks while their hands and arms were tied behind their backs. I recognized their faces. Were they trying to resist? Perhaps! But if what came out of their contorted lips were screams, the strength of their breaths exceeded by little the feeble bleating of sheep destined for slaughter. Thereupon, the ropes with which they were restrained were thrown toward the twin ship, as if in an exchange between jugglers. Suddenly, the two ships, which almost collided, slowly began to move away from each other. And those bodies, limp up until that moment, were stretched beyond limit and, after a few heaves, torn asunder, ripped apart alive amid the jubilation of the crowd. I have often wondered what might have passed through the minds of those young men in the face of their depraved end. I wished to believe that, distracted by the hilarity of the rabble, they might have found in ire and contempt a respite, an escape from pain. Then, however, I come back to the sight of their wide-open eyes, their body parts becoming detached, and every illusion, every word giveth way to silence. Who knows? Perhaps one day, from those same watery depths in which they plunged, shredded to pieces, their spirits—stronger than oblivion, more persistent than hate—will slip into the bodies of the Mayan father or of his angel Michael. One thing, however, I have learned, owing to the clairvoyance of the dreams: although my body may cease to be, my soul will rupture the fabric of time, and once again, Tommaso will rise.

~ 6 ~

Leyla

Saint Luke University, Saranac Lake,
New York—September 2007

Another disappointment, another fatal blow, another humiliation to endure like a symbolic badge of honor. In the very
same instant that Michael and Pablo's gazes intersected, a
gust of wind, the kind that precedes hurricanes, made Leyla
jump out of her chair. She knew that her life would be
upended, and the fragile harbor she had laboriously created
would be destroyed. But it was already too late to run for
shelter. "Life can never stop," she thought, "and what can you
do when the tide drags you to the bottom except float to
the surface and fight not to drown? You have to conquer the
waves, one stroke at a time, take a deep breath. That's all
anyone can do." Lost in these fantasies, Leyla continued

to speak, albeit distractedly, without taking her eyes off Michael's essay, taking in with a third cerebral eye, the sometimes animated, sometimes hungry looks passing between the two men. She would have liked to remind Michael about the reason for their meeting, calling his attention back to the few pages hiding her face, like a sniper's barricade. She would have liked to blurt out, "If you want, I can go into the next room and give you two a bit of privacy." Instead, she declared almost yelling, "These theories of yours on the cloak of Caravaggio's Madonna, Michael, are truly innovative," dragging out that last word as if it were a steamship whistle. Michael was immediately brought back down to earth by the shrill sound of his teacher's voice. In the meantime, Leyla forged ahead, specifying that she had found his reflections on the painting promising and original— "extremely original," she emphasized—and that it couldn't have been coincidental that the Madonna of Mercy was represented by the artist as a breastfeeding Madonna. Then she pressed on, "Because it is true that in the figurative tradition, the Madonna of Mercy is usually represented with a sheltering cloak within which it's possible to see the souls of purgatory all crammed and crushed together, as they wait for forgiveness, but it is also true that over these same reformed souls, this Madonna—in living memory—typically pours a redemptive maternal milk." "And instead," she continued a little deceitfully, "starting with your brilliant research and— why not?—pushing beyond it, this Madonna by Caravaggio does not seem to be interested in anything but herself and her child attached to her breast." Leyla knew well that this uninterrupted jabbering, which she was using to cover up her embarrassment, these weird intentions that she was attributing to the protagonists of *The Seven Works of Mercy* did not come from the artist but from her own sick fantasy.

At the same time, what else could she say? What explanation could she offer? Her brain was running at a hundred miles an hour. Michael was nodding and asking himself for the first time about this egotistical and visceral feeling that Leyla was assigning to the Madonna because he felt it well up inside himself. He understood it in the way one understands a mission, an indisputable choice. It was the kind of love that divided the entire world into two irreconcilable factions: allies and enemies.

Two Months Later

The baby was squirming furiously in her belly, and every kick was a shock to the edifice of fragile certainties and convictions that Leyla had painstakingly built up over the years. In these moments, it was not only her insipid mask of respectability that fell but also every layer of her personality. How could she have called herself a feminist and then tolerate placing herself at the service of a male who had not yet been born? What insufferable hypocrisy had she shown when criticizing her female colleagues, who were unable to balance family and work, when for weeks just managing to get out of bed to prepare breakfast without bursting into tears was her greatest achievement, proof of a successful day? She realized that this progressive exhaustion of hers was not entirely attributable to her pregnancy. At every kick of her child, at every impulse crushed to pieces, at every tear flowing down her face, a new memory resurfaced. But was it a memory or a fantasy, the hallucination of a sick mind? And why did these memories unsettle her so much? Were they shattering the little world that she had so carefully constructed? Was it because they transformed this baby that was intended to save her into an evil and vengeful elf? In the final analysis, the only thing to avenge were the lies that she had always told herself, those abuses she had shoved into a dusty old closet and, after years and years, had pulled out all wrinkled and faded. She squeezed her eyes shut and saw once again the image of her father, the caress that went too deep and that slipped from her knee under her checked skirt, and then that other caress on Christmas Day. It had stopped at the height of her tiny thigh, stopped right there. "But what if instead. . . ." And why did that hand linger? Why did it not let go of her left leg? She still felt it there, as if welded to her skin. And then a new shiver passed through her body, a tingling sensation that perhaps was nothing more than a temporary dizziness. She would have liked to amputate her leg, push aside that hand forever, but by now, the hand had climbed up from the leg to her swollen uterus and from there to her neck, strangling her, taking her breath away.

By now, she was in her eighth month. The monster was growing in her ill-suited belly and was faithful to her. She felt it; it was the ogre that would do her justice. She hadn't imagined that it would be so cumbersome, so exhausting, and because of this, she continuously assailed her doctors with different worries, showing up at the hospital, at all times of day or night because she felt alarmed by some new anxiety, some new fear, a vague symptom that the internet said could get worse. The doctors continued to repeat that all of this was normal and that, of course, the baby was a little heavier than the average but that they could still wait a few weeks before deciding to do a cesarean. "And the tiredness? Do you know a pregnant woman who isn't tired?" they added, mocking her. She remembered that as a little girl, she felt enchanted as she listened to the stories of the happy pregnancies of grand-mothers and great-aunts and that these were pregnancies lived among friends and relatives—moments marked by the prayers of a muezzin. As a career woman, being pregnant in the United States, was a whole other story. It meant counting the hospital visits to avoid exorbitant costs, your family far away, wishing for the kindness of acquaintances and strangers who, except for offering some polite smiles, would rarely come to the rescue. Above all, being a pregnant woman in the United States meant having three or four weeks of leave and making do by yourself for all the rest. In Leyla's case, the workload—teaching, research—remained perfectly unchanged, and there were many times she wondered if her academic determination was none other than a kind of obtuseness, if it might not be better to give it up before her dismissal for negligence. "For the position of associate professor, you will have to come, if not with an already published and reviewed book, at least with an offer of publication," the dean had made clear at their last meeting. Yet it was already a great deal if she could devote herself to her article on *The Seven Works of Mercy* since in all other respects, her days were basically reduced to a relay race between classes, housekeeping, and hospital visits. Recently, however, she had come into possession of a collection of essays that could perhaps push her past the stalemate in which she was idling. But read it all? Read it thoroughly? She didn't know if it was realistic. Still, she had managed to read the piece signed by the Pio Monte archivist, and from this, new information had emerged about the founders of the chapel. In particular, not only had the archivist rediscovered the true date of the founding of the confraternity, fixing it at August 17, 1601, but she had talked at length about the assemblies initiated and organized every Friday by the members of the association. For a while now, Leyla had been wondering if the painting might have an astrological meaning. The discovery by the archivist helped corroborate this hypothesis of hers. In fact, rummaging through the papers of the Neapolitan intellectual circles of the seventeenth century, Leyla had learned that it was common for the members of the Pio Monte to attribute more importance to astrology than to religion. In other words, Giovanni Manso and the other friends of Caravaggio were convinced that the stars influenced their lives more than divinities and saints. It was not impossible, therefore, that the choice of Friday as the day of their meetings might indicate a thinly disguised cult of Venus, whether star or heavenly power, and Leyla started having the feeling she could discover the painting's definitive clue in some reading from that period. However, to prove these theories of hers would unfortunately necessitate more time, probably a trip to Italy, while at the moment, the only move she could envision was to a hospital a thousand miles away and that only in a case where they realized that a birth at the local hospital would be equivalent to a death sentence. Every now and then, she asked herself if she should contact her parents, ask them to help her, make it so they could be there at the moment of the birth. But the memories that were resurfacing as of late prevented her from calling. In the meantime, she began to compile imaginary lists of names, wondering which was the most suitable for this baby boy without grandparents, without a father, and practically without roots. She was convinced that assigning a name corresponded to dispensing a destiny, a way of confronting life. She hoped her unborn child would be as willful and combative in the world as he seemed to be in her womb. Then, on reflection, she told herself that she would like it if his willfulness were not of the deaf and masculine kind but the pliant and compassionate willfulness of women. The world she had come to know required the prayer and the sword, cunning and madness.

A sound surfaced in her consciousness, and in that instant, she found a first solution to the painting's enigma but also a destiny for her future child and protector. "Tommaso Campanella," she said out loud. "I will call him Tommaso."

A Few Weeks Later

She saw the blood flowing between her legs and, along with the blood, a gelatinous and phosphorescent slime of the same color as the neon light coming from the television when left on in the middle of the night. She rummaged nervously around in the kitchen drawers looking for the phone number of the doctor, dumping out everything that she had haphazardly thrown in there months ago: receipts, unopened bills, her watch that had stopped and she had never repaired. It was a waste of time. The number was not in the drawer as she well knew. She began to scream. It was not pain. It was anger. She jumped into the car and drove toward the hospital, terrified by who she was, by the idea of losing control. She repeated over and over to herself, "Concentrate, Leyla. Hang in there." When she finally got to the hospital, she must have been white as a ghost. In her haste, she had forgotten to wash or brush her hair, and all of this contributed to the effect of urgency that she wished to communicate. A plump nurse in reception invited her to take a seat and gave her a glass of water. Leyla wondered whether it was normal that no one was interested in the slime easily visible on her leg, the same leg her father used to hold. . . . "Don't fret. The doctor will be here momentarily," the nurse exclaimed, perhaps sensing her distress. "He's at his nephew's baptism, but he said that he would set off for the hospital immediately after dessert." The nurse spoke one sentence after another and Leyla had no idea how to respond. She felt bewildered by this explanation that seemed lacking in logic and compassion. She lost her patience and shouted, "Call Pablo. Call the father!" and threw her cell phone at the nurse. She herself was taken aback by this brusque reaction of hers but was able to distract herself by focusing on the hairnet keeping together the nurse's hair, and then the hairstyles of the other patients in the waiting room, all clearly immigrants. "Where have they all come from?" she asked herself. "Where have they been hiding up till now?" The nurse, already on the phone, was trying to call the absent father in hopes of relieving herself—and as quickly as possible—of this patient on the verge of a breakdown. But what was she, Leyla, expecting from Pablo? Why had she made the nurse call him? Perhaps she was just feeling the need to make him understand what it meant to be a woman, shake him out of his much-too-easy kindliness, teach him—as no one had yet done—that there are no actions without consequences. It was at that moment that she heard the train passing through Saranac Lake, with that long whistle that merged with her desperate shouts, shouts similar to those of dreams in which no one can hear you. The train by now was inside her and crossing through her, tearing through her. Suddenly, she lost consciousness and fainted.

Saint Luke University, Saranac Lake, New York—
March 2008, Four Months Later

Living with Pablo had been the best choice, the most practical, thanks also to the fact that his cheerful lunacy compensated for and made his masculine ineptitude a little more tolerable. This did not change the fact that after four months of living together, Leyla went to bed every night a little before

10:00—worn out, distraught, and incapable of uttering a single word. She was forced into this life of togetherness for the good of the child because Pablo had implored her and because, not being able to tolerate his continuous whining, she had preferred to give in to him immediately rather than see him prostrate himself in nauseating declarations of eternal love. In short, she had accepted him and his presence for convenience. At the birth of the baby, she had received a note signed by her colleagues in the department, who, on wishing her a swift recovery, urged her, rather underhandedly, to return to teaching her classes as soon as possible and, in other words, "not to relax too much." She had laughed at the idea that pregnancy should be treated like a cold from which she could "speedily" recover. However, on rereading the note, she made up her mind: "Pablo will be useful." He was a young man, true, not exactly a model parent, and yet she asked herself, "Could he do worse than a university student turned nanny?" Pablo, for his part, hurried over each and every time she gave him the opportunity to take care of his son, and moreover, she concluded, "It won't cost me a penny." In the meantime, her parents had also come to the rescue. They had shown up right after the birth, demonstrating an unexpected and somewhat annoying zeal. "We have the right to be grandparents," they had cried during a Skype conversation, begging her to forgive them the mysterious faults she evidently imputed to them. Leyla, who had fought all her life to keep them at bay, felt for the first time willing to compromise. And as if with a flick of a magic wand, that slight opening caused a real breakthrough. Surprised with herself, she started wondering whether the birth of Tommaso had contributed to her capitulation, if the appearance of the baby had swallowed the resentment that she had been chewing on for years. She was certain of one thing: she was leaking submissiveness from all her pores. And she was sinking deeper and deeper.

Aiyla and Erkan, Leyla's parents, had arrived at the beginning of the spring. In the last of a long series of telephone negotiations, Leyla had approved a visit, "provided it was short." At the same time, she had also specified that the guest room was yet to be furnished and that since she would every day be engaged with classes and meetings, "they should bring something to do with them." This small concession, this minuscule opening on the part of their daughter was enough for Aiyla and Erkan, her parents now grandparents, to pack and depart complete with weapons and baggage. Fifteen hours later, parked in the small tree-filled courtyard in front of Leyla's house, they had unloaded such an enormous quantity of parcels and packages that Leyla was afraid they wanted to stay forever. If she hadn't abhorred all theories of the absurd, she would have suspected that Erkan and Aiyla were fleeing from a house in flames and seeing their grandson was an excuse to acquire a roof over their heads. She wondered when exactly they had decided to become grandparents. In spite of this, while pushing aside the curtains and watching them from a distance, she realized suddenly that five years had passed since they had seen each other last and that this interval of time, otherwise negligible, had left indelible traces on their bodies. She barely recognized the elderly couple, bumbling and out of breath, as they groped toward her door. Actually, upon waving to them from behind her window, she was overwhelmed by a sharp sense of estrangement. Aiyla and Erkan reminded her of one of those films in which an unknown species of aliens take on the features of a dear friend or sibling but with a coldness and precision that betrays their true identity. They were already at the threshold, ready to ring the bell, when Leyla, all smiles, opened the door: after all, the science fiction had already degenerated into farce, and this transference of consciousness, alien or human, turned out to be so clumsy and inelegant as to produce in her a sentiment of heart-rending compassion.

In the weeks after their arrival, Aiyla and Erkan stayed at home, taking care of the baby with a professionalism that bordered on obsessiveness. They alternated this job with Pablo, with whom they also shared a sense of collaboration that as the days passed became a friendship at first cordial, then almost loving. Like in a vaudeville show, Leyla, who, thanks to her work, allowed this bizarre team to function seamlessly, ended up being relegated to the role of castrating girlfriend, ungrateful daughter, disaffected mother; in other words, she became everyone's enemy. And although she realized how unhealthy this family dynamic was, she truly did not know how to undo it. But she was certain of one thing: she would never be able to find the right words to provoke a change in direction. So she took a piece of paper and began to jot down a series of possible excuses: "I would like to furnish and decorate the guest room so that on your next visit it will be more comfortable," or "Perhaps this is the moment for me and Pablo to spend some time by ourselves with the baby," or possibly, "It would be nice to give Tommaso a little brother." But there was no hope for her! What would her face look like when she would spit out these lies? She would come off as mean. It would make things worse. One evening, coming home later than usual, she found all the lights off. Her mother had left only the light of the stove hood on as she did during her high school years, when Leyla, still quite young, went out dancing and returned at sunrise. Leyla understood that they were actually in bed, and to treat herself to a moment of freedom, she opened a bottle of pinot grigio. She slipped off her skirt, which, quite comfortable in the morning, after fifteen hours of work, had begun to feel like a straitjacket. And so, holding the bottle by the neck and in her tights only, she slowly made her way from the kitchen toward the living room. The first thing that struck her, though, was a strange purple glow that unwound across the walls like the tentacles of an octopus. Then, after a few seconds, she was able to make out the silhouette of her father in the dark. And there he was, sprawled out on the couch, hypnotized by the screen of his computer on mute. From the angle of the room where she was standing, it wasn't possible for her to see what he was looking at. She was not even sure that he was still awake. Even so, once she moved toward the arch that gave access to the room, she began to piece together the fragments of the mosaic. Methodical and almost indifferent, her father was using his left hand to keep his flannel pajama bottoms lowered, and with the other, he was grabbing himself and mechanically masturbating. Leyla was afraid to move. She would have liked to disappear. It was only when her father turned toward her, his vacant gaze on her, his hand still clutching his erect penis that her throat felt strangled. She gagged, and her sight grew dim; it was only then that she realized, as she recovered her vision, her father lay on the ground unconscious, blood on his face, glass fragments all over the floor. Leyla headed toward the telephone in a decisive manner. "I need help. I need an ambulance . . . immediately."

In the hospital, sitting next to her father, Leyla wondered whether that instinctive and mystifying reaction of hers had made her a strong woman. Over the years, she had come to believe that being strong meant not feeling the obligation to ask for permission, but a subtle line between an essential gesture and an abusive one persisted. She looked around her. Was her mother strong? Had her grandmother been strong? Stoic, certainly, examples of an old-fashioned patience, yes, but strong? And she herself, who had risked sending her blameless father into an irreversible coma, had she been strong? She realized that she had been running away all her life, and the urge to obliterate an unpleasant scene was nothing else but another attempt at denial. When had all this begun? When had she learned to recognize the rancid smell of danger, the alarm bell that made you run like hell? It had to have been that day, as a child, when her brother had disappeared forever, for the weeks and years that followed. The death of her brother had been something about which no one ever spoke—a silence to protect. And it was during the following weeks that Leyla had learned to be elsewhere, to seek out oxygen away from that house, beyond its flat and dull temporality. Her love for research had probably begun over those weeks. Studying another century meant living elsewhere, becoming untraceable, losing oneself along other streets. How had her brother died? Where had he ended up? At the time, Leyla was twelve. She should have remembered. Despite this, if she wanted to tell the story, she wouldn't know where to begin. The story, as best as she could reconstruct it, was one of two parents and a son, unquestionably the darling of the family, heading for the lake on an early summer trip. Then the return of only the parents, many hours later, at night, two grief-stricken creatures, two instead of three. No one ever spoke of death. There had been an accident. And yet, Leyla had instinctively sensed that her brother's disappearance was forever. In the months that followed, during the silent and empty days, she was able to interpret the inappropriate attention, which her father paid her, as a sort of confession. It seemed as if without uttering a word, the man was whispering to her, "Leyla, don't you understand? This has all been an act to release me from the other two. This has enabled me to be alone with you." And while her mother was behaving like a widow in her second stage of grief, the frequency of her father's caresses had to reassure her that they would not take her to the lake. Thinking about all this in the hospital, as she stood before the shrunken and practically lifeless body of her father, Leyla wondered if that brother had actually existed, if that fondling on the part of her father was nothing other than a slightly morbid plea for affection. She guessed that growing old did not make anyone wiser or better. Aging meant allowing the body to free itself, to forget, to become truly strong.

What had occurred with her father had made the curtain come down on a phase of her life. As in a Shakespearian play, it would have to end quickly and with the death of all the protagonists. Saranac Lake could not suffice anymore, and the exile she had imposed on herself for too many years was at an end. Once her father recovered from his brain trauma, Leyla dictated the exact date of their departure and stuffed in the boxes from her first move the hundreds of knickknacks that they had left in every corner of her house. To avoid her parents staying any longer, Leyla herself pushed them—practically carrying them—into the old rust bucket they had originally arrived in. "Let them sink back into the hole out of which they had crawled." And that was that. As soon as the car disappeared around the corner, she walked back home, repeating to herself that all she had now to deal with was Pablo: he was the last tie to untie. But she hadn't even crossed the threshold when her rage turned into dejection. Pablo was staring at her with his usual hangdog look. He seemed to have guessed that he was to be the next victim in this Soviet-style purge of hers and, instinctively following the orders she hadn't yet communicated to him, headed toward Tommaso's room. The first thing Leyla noticed when she finally reached him was how he communicated with his son. Pablo's serious tone reminded her of an epic novel. It was the tone with which Hector must have spoken to Astyanax before his last duel. Then she saw the suitcase already packed, placed on the ground only a few centimeters from the crib. Leyla's left hand would have liked to take Pablo by the lapel and force him to stay. The other hand, however, was holding the door of the room wide open, as if to say, "Then go. Go now." She never knew what Pablo had whispered to his son, but she sensed in that moment that the spell that connected Tommaso to Pablo came from another time and that it would come back to haunt her. The self-love, a feeling of which Pablo had seemed incapable, had been passed from father to son. And while all this was going on around her, Leyla understood that it was impossible for her to interrupt the flow of events. Here was a destiny that no one, not Pablo, certainly not little Tommaso, and least of all herself, could escape. When the last word slid into Tommaso's ear, Pablo picked up the suitcase from the floor, placed a light kiss on Leyla's cheek, and left without looking backward. Leyla softly whispered these words: "We will never see him again." An icy-cold shiver rose up along her spine.

With the house now empty, Leyla felt lost in the middle of a rocky desert. As if hallucinating, she saw the walls of her house part like the waters of the Red Sea. Unfortunately, beyond them she could not make out any promised land. Instead, she mentally fixated on the long wilderness of days to come, resembling a row of cards lined up as far as the eye could see. "Not all prisons are narrow," she commented to herself. She would hold on for a few more months, maybe a few years, move in a systematic and orderly fashion, in the worst case, waiting until she was given or denied the title of associate professor. In either case, she would collect her things and those of her child and leave for London, or New York, or any other city. She sighed. She had a moment of hesitation, and then she had a sudden insignificant epiphany. She had often heard people talk of New York as "the Big Apple," but she had never paused to ponder the meaning of the expression. Now, all at once, it came to her. New York was the big apple because there was something for everyone, because you could bite into it, slice it to bits, without preventing the city from continuing to grow, to swell, feeding off the same hunger that wished to annihilate it. All of a sudden, she detected a glimmer of hope. Let them maul her. Let them reduce her to nothing. It was only a matter of a couple of years at the most. Like New York, she would fall. She would get back up. She would become colossal. At any rate, she couldn't see any other way to live.

PART 3

Thomas Eakins, *Nude, Playing Pipes*, ca. 1883.

Caravaggio, *The Denial of Saint Peter*, 1610.

~ 7 ~

Leyla

New York, New York—September 2010

Against all expectations, she had been promoted to associate professor. Now that she had reached her goal, however, the challenge to keep her in Saranac Lake was no longer there. And so in a matter of a few weeks, she organized her departure. The decision that she had taken two years before, when she threw Pablo out, would become reality: after a quick round of goodbyes, she gathered her things and left town forever. As she descended the stairs of the bus at the Port Authority Station, she was well aware that moving to New York with a toddler was more reckless than heroic, and yet, she remembered when, as a young girl, she had disembarked at the same terminal on Forty-Second Street, suitcase in hand and a feeling of exaltation that others would have called hope. Years later, makeup could no longer deceive. Like Cinderella at the end of the ball, New York was stripped of its splendor. The grayness, the pollution, and that acrid smell that characterizes all cities that grow up too quickly had finally got the better of the urban utopia of its founders. And yet, today just as yesterday, the light of morning passed through the micro granules of dust and suspended them in the air like balloons at a children's party. Leyla started walking along Eighth Avenue, uncertain about what to do. She didn't want to take a cab because she was sure they would get stuck in traffic. Yet the idea of taking the subway at rush hour, Tommaso on her back and her suitcase in tow, sent her into a state of exhaustion and despair. She froze on the sidewalk awaiting an idea that would save her from paralysis, while her attention oscillated between Tower 39 on one side and the Bear Building on the other side. And it was there, as she pondered her options, that she was almost knocked down by a troop of young women who surrounded her on every side, like the two skyscrapers from the twenties ground into anonymity by the more recent and imposing structures. At the same time, like the two gilded-age buildings with their by now run-down facades, she knew she had precedence over those girls in stiletto heels. Or at least so she believed in the moment. With confidence, then, she whistled for the first taxi that passed, got into the car, and hastily handed the driver the address of the Second Avenue apartment where she would be staying for practically nothing. Upon the death of her grandmother, in fact, Leyla and her cousins had inherited a two-room cubbyhole on the Lower East Side, and while waiting for an agreement and a lawyer who would organize the succession, Leyla had managed to get them to consent to her staying there temporarily. The apartment was not large. Leyla would have to sleep in the only bedroom with Tommaso, making the other room a dining room/living room/office. The kitchen was in a state of lamentable neglect. The bathroom had been installed at the time of construction and never refurbished. Just before dying, the old lady had managed to provide those two rooms with an image of decent functionality, and although the apartment had been closed up for months, thus absorbing the odors of the Venezuelan restaurant below, Leyla trusted she would be able to create an inviting space in a matter of a few weeks. Before devoting herself to the apartment, however, she had to contact the babysitter suggested by Lauren—a longtime friend, who, after marrying a rich banker, had moved from Harlem to the Upper East Side, discarding her ragged clothes and effortlessly transforming herself into a trophy wife. Leyla prayed deep in her heart that the babysitter could make herself immediately available because her work interview was scheduled for Monday morning and because Lauren, as much as she was a generous adviser, would hardly be able to tackle the responsibility of a toddler (not that Lauren was a bad person, but to tell the truth, she could barely take care of her own children). In any event, Leyla was certain that rescheduling her interview with the museum staff was not really an option. That they had contacted her for this position as archivist was already a miracle, maybe even a mistake on their part. She didn't dare imagine how she would be able to make ends meet if this interview didn't work out. So, while making a mental list of things to do, she vacuumed the house and scoured the bathroom tiles without really knowing whether she was fighting the dirt, the dilapidation, or her own stubborn passion for living. It was an endless week. With time, however, she had developed a technique to defend herself from the panic attacks, which, coming in waves, continued to overwhelm her: it didn't matter if on the street, in the bath, or in the aisles of a supermarket, all she had to do was to position herself in one direction—the real or imaginary direction leading to her son, Tommaso. From there, she then gazed right into the eyes of the child, and in a whisper, imperceptible to the human ear, she solemnly promised him that his mother would survive, that she would never abandon him, be she blind, crippled, or even dead.

A Month Later

She had taken it in her hands with the same caution she would have used with a relic in decomposition. For no apparent reason, it reminded her of a moment when, as a little girl, she had been fascinated by a forget-me-not—by the flower itself but also by its name. Perhaps because the letter seemed to have accidentally slipped into her mailbox, perhaps because of the naturalness with which she had picked it up, Leyla couldn't help but think about the audacity and the actual time that it had taken to compose a handwritten letter and then to send it by regular mail. As for her, she wouldn't have been able to say when she had last sent or received a postcard. She read the name of the sender on the envelope and a clown-like grin distorted her face due a little to nostalgia and a little to nervousness. They had a son together, and even though their farewell was entirely her doing with no strings attached, there were still moments when she secretly felt tormented by how easily Pablo had abandoned them and moved on. Not that she ever considered Pablo prone to practical concerns or asking questions about, for example, a first ear infection or the inexplicable childhood fevers, and certainly she knew him well enough to know that the transience of life interested him less than a night at the bar. And here was Pablo writing her a letter, "a little letter"—she sardonically laughed—of such coy artificiality that Leyla hesitated to open it, fearing she might rip or damage it in some way. She decided to get a knife and open the envelope from above, imitating the delicacy of the sender. On the other hand, she thought, perhaps this piece of paper was the only contact Tommaso would ever have with his father, one of the only remnants that she could show him when he was older. She drew out the letter, and the whiff of lavender emanating from the paper further annoyed her. She felt officially played for a sucker.

Dear Leyla,

I waited a long time before writing this letter, but I did not want you to find out from others what I am about to tell you. At any rate, for you, no matter what, I'm always in the wrong. The day you threw me out, my life—the way I had imagined it—ended. It would be easy to talk of depression, to tell you that crashing into a tree at two hundred miles an hour seemed to me the only thing to do on the most difficult days. It would be easy and would only be partly true. That lack of meaning was, despite myself, also interrupted by flashes of hope, moments in which I thought of giving up everything and imploring you to take me on as a babysitter, the cleaner, a rag to use whenever needed. But we both know that in the long months of our cohabitation, I wasn't much more. I was lost. I often told myself that it was all my fault and that almost certainly it had to be me that was wrong. I don't believe that it will be news to you if I add to this letter what you already know about what happened, or what you perhaps had already intuited before we did . . . I mean between me and Michael. And yes, there was something between us, but to define exactly what this "something" was might be difficult even for someone like me, who was never a participant all the way. In the beginning, during the first secret meetings with Michael, I felt shame, and not because I was sleeping with a man—I have never cared much for stereotypes like this. What I was really ashamed of was the betrayal in relation to you, a pregnant woman who deserved my full attention, my devotion as father. And yet, whenever I tried to forgive myself in my heart, to approach you, you drove me away like a mosquito. At those times, I often feared that you felt a physical repugnance for me, that the pregnancy had even altered your taste in men—in other words, that I was no longer useful for anything. And every time I sank into the darkest desperation, Michael was always there, welcoming, silent, ready to open himself up to me at the slightest touch. In the beginning, Michael represented sin for me, a revenge against you, but then, over time, I understood that within this perverse dynamic of ours, Michael was the only one who paid a price. Today, my only regret is not that of having abandoned Tommaso— that child is only yours (you conceived him in your mind even before knowing me, and my semen only served a rather paltry function). My only regret is having preferred the two of you to Michael, having allowed him to slip through my fingers, having chased a dream that wasn't even mine. I have therefore decided to take what little hope I have left and squeeze it into a fist. I have decided to go after Michael and beg him to be mine as he has never been before. I do not hope for your blessing, but I know that you will understand. Forgive my slowness, my cowardice. And if one day Tommaso asks you about his father, tell him a better story, tell him about a better man.

Leyla put the letter back in the envelope and stuck it into a drawer. She ruminated, "How good he feels! How much he likes himself!" A few minutes later, she took it out again and furiously threw it into the trash, the whole thing, without tearing it up. And with the letter, she felt she had also thrown Pablo away.

The autumn at the Metropolitan Museum turned out to be more exciting than Leyla could have imagined. Initially, she had accepted the work out of necessity. However, over time, she came to realize that relieved of the endless flow of futile e-mails sent by students and colleagues, she could, right in the museum itself, resume her earlier research. Among other things, the job at the archives guaranteed her immediate access both to the exhibited works as well as to those kept in storage, works that would otherwise be impossible to see. Of course, there were still moments in which, overcome again by her indomitable illness, she gave herself entirely up to panic, others in which she would crouch down in the toilet cubicles, and between sobs, gag over the impossibility of being both a mother and career woman. But they were brief and infrequent breakdowns. All things considered, since the move to New York, her days seemed to have regained color, density, and meaning. The autumn already had the flavor of a new season, and Leyla told herself, sometimes feeling contentment and sometimes a sense of mischief, "Maybe it's just because the people of Saranac Lake are so different, or maybe it's the electricity of New York." Nevertheless, it wasn't only the energy of New Yorkers that have spurred her to pick up her abandoned research. The *Denial of Saint Peter*, attributed to Caravaggio and on full view in the rooms of European painting, had exerted a magnetic pull on her right from her first days in the museum. She had passed by it one morning when she was looking for a shortcut between the rooms, and to her, who perhaps had not been this close to a Caravaggio in years, those knotted fingers turned toward the chest seemed to be saying, "Look at me again, return to me." The moment caused her an unconscious shiver. That same evening, she had returned to gaze at the painting. With difficulty would she have been able to compose her present life out of the series of humiliations and compromises that had constrained her for so long. Making a quick gesture with her hand, as if she were waving goodbye to a relative or friend from the balustrade of a departing ship, she swept away the pile of memories that was still linking her to the past. However, from that day, she often came back to that painting, reproaching herself for having too often preferred catalogs to the direct observation of the work. Something about the formulation of the color and the detail unequivocally juxtaposed the painting of the *Denial* with other canvases of the same period. The soldier's helmet, for example, recalled the one from the *Liberation of Saint Peter*, now attributed to Caracciolo and painted for the Pio Monte della Misericordia. The position of the hands and a certain approximation in the brushwork brought it closer to the *Martyrdom of Saint Ursula*, Caravaggio's final painting, with the difference that whereas Peter pointed his fingers at his chest in renunciation of his faith, the young Ursula used the same hand gesture to willingly receive the arrow shot into her abdomen by her depraved executioner. The comparison between the two works forced Leyla to wonder who was the most meritorious: the apostle, and father of the church, determined to survive, even for just one day, to be a witness to the Good News of Christ, or the tenacious female saint, who, like every young girl, was foolishly proud in the defense of her virginity. This was a choice that included her as well: move forward, putting aside her own wounded pride, or set herself up as the martyr of her own destiny. She thought back to Tommaso Campanella, to how he had pretended to be mad to escape death and risk oblivion, to what he had done to go on living, and writing.

— 8 —

Tommaso Campanella

Naples, Kingdom of Naples—July 1600:
Imprisonment at Castel Nuovo

Should I surrender myself to death like Cleopatra or resist until my final breath? No incarceration hath been more painful, more terribly revealing than this last Neapolitan imprisonment of mine. To kill myself would be easy, egotistical, painless. It would require a good measure of faith in the intelligence of history and in future generations. I lack this certainty, or else I am just not ready to choose death. Unlike Cleopatra or Cato, I am well acquainted, alas too well, with the morals and the memory of my fellow citizens, the sins, the vain ambitions of ungodly men without ideals. These modern times have deprived us of more reasonable hopes! Thus, by means of expedients of every sort, I will pretend to be mad every time the net around me tightens. I do not know any other way to resist. To the world, Campanella is mad and those shall be damned who, by advocating for his death, will wish to deny him the possibility of repentance. Have not our laws determined that it is a mortal sin to condemn he who is of unsound mind? Shall our governors continue to slavishly follow writings that have never been placed under the scrutiny of judgment and reason? Just as David and Solon before me, I will resort to the theater of madness to avoid the aegis of the tyrant. Like Brutus, who, before the slaughter of sons and relatives, knew how to feign mental illness to pierce the heart of the despot, I, too, will flee the machinations of Satan and then crush him like a viper. I know that God is at my side, and so my friends who resort to a thousand stratagems to send me missives and money in exchange for prophecies and horoscopes. Furthermore, if I have learned anything through this period of imprisonment, it is that the power of the will, assisted by the stars, can suffice to determine by itself victory or perdition. I had an inkling of this, the first time during the forty hours of torture in which they crushed my legs and arms. I made use of this when they interrogated me, my back suspended at a finger's distance from the wooden dagger that could have stabbed me. My every moment of lightness was in fact marked by a cut, a scar. These, too, I wear with pride. They represent physical weaknesses, moments of relaxation. As for the spirit, it did not bend. Never, over the course of these years, have I ever yielded to the confession of heresy that they so tenaciously wished to extract from me, and even less did they succeed in compelling me to admit that my madness was feigned, if one can speak of madness in this cesspool of reason. And thus I am still in chains but still miraculously alive—and blessed is he, the doctor of the prison, a lamb among wolves, a shaman capable of separating battered flesh from live flesh. But all is not lost! A horoscope that Manso sought from me to establish the most propitious date for the foundation of his Pio Monte alerted me to the entrance of Venus in Cancer during the night of August 17. May the star of love, therefore, be able to break the chains of Mars, and may the virginal veil of *Caritas* be able to discover what reason obscures. "Tommaso," I say to myself, "do not let thy guard down," and my eyes are burning embers in the night, an infinite night that seems to never end, a night that will make us forget the gentle touch of day.

Naples, Kingdom of Naples—July 1604: Imprisonment at Castel Sant'Elmo

I have been transferred from Castel Nuovo to the prison of Saint Elmo. Tommaso, the prisoner, is moving from house to house, and in spite of himself, the world out there continues to spin because—and of this I am certain—the world is indeed spinning. Having reached the top of this hill, I felt for the first time in three years a renewal of strength, the invigoration of my dream. And it is thanks to these new energies that I began to write a short poetic dialogue, which I then called *The City of the Sun*. I know that there will be some who, upon reading it, will treat it like a utopian pamphlet, those who will see it as a sketch of an ideal city, the vagary of a fool. However, I did feel the need to make it understood that this city can truly exist and that I, moreover, had the good fortune to live there. Because when pushing the vision beyond the walls that encircle it—whether a real prison, like my own, or an intangible structure—it is possible to train the inner eye to see beyond worldly appearances. By using this technique, one can vault over the ramparts that keep us incarcerated and treasure, although at a distance, a community that, separated from the world, hath known how to cast off the superfluous and share the rest. From the top of our prison, it is possible to detect the sky but also the sinister labyrinth of our cities, the bruised and battered bodies within them, as well as what these enclaves could potentially be. From here to Saint Elmo, for example, I can see the old Decumanus road, the statue of Nile, and the living, breathing body of Naples. From here and only from here, the sun and its stars guide me, speak to me, comfort me. He who enters these cells and whose soul hath been stifled sees nothing else but walls defaced by nonsensical scratches and scribbles. And on the other hand, for those who know how to be transported beyond the veneer of things, there are magnificent paintings on our walls, representing an encyclopedia of knowledge. Of this I speak and of more in my *City of the Sun.* I tell of what I believe myself, what I feel or what I believe to be feeling. I recount a way of life that we have known and forgotten, and sometimes I wonder who is really in prison: those of us who are up here, or those in the city below? While we follow draconian rules and norms, it is in fact possible for us, the citizens of the City of the Sun, to give and receive a pure and ever-changing affection. We are not, of course, rich! But these modest resources of ours preserve us from insolence and arrogance. In the meantime, the needs that our orchards satisfy protect each one of us from cowardice, thievery, and conspiracy. We fully count on the fact that every food is available to all and sundry. On the towers high above our city walls, our astrologers observe the stars, instruct us on how to behave, and show us the right path. In our city, the two sexes have equal rights, are equal in dignity, and if sometimes we lighten the burden of women, it is only out of respect for their aptitudes and predispositions. Let it be clear: the women of this city of ours are as strong as Amazons and as clever as hawks. They therefore abhor the use of cosmetics and face powder that in Naples enjoy so much success among noblewomen and whores alike (wretched women, these latter, forced to cover up a precarious state of health that is none other than a debilitating sickness of the soul). There are other customs that make us proud and for which, notwithstanding the scandal, we feel no shame. In fact, word hath spread that along with food and possessions, we also share beds, which is in itself true and not because we wish to be considered an orgiastic sect, or a cult, as infamy would have, but because within these walls, sexuality, separate from love, hath a reproductive purpose alone. As such, then, it is at everyone's disposal. It seems to me that if we knowingly breed dogs or horses to preserve the purity of the race, why wouldn't we do the same for the progeny of God? Love, then, is something other. Love is a gesture, a garland fashioned in secret. Love doth not cling, or clutch, or lick. And to all those who call us heretics, we answer that they have lost the way of God, that if they knew how to read, they would find no discrepancy between the book of nature and the word of Christ, that they should draw on His light, thanks to the light of our Sun, a living temple, father of nature, life, and the soul of all things, supreme intelligence, sole foundation, immovable center.

What is happening now? Why are these lights extinguished? Where can I exit? On which side is the Sun? I am cold. I am afraid. I am a worm that slithers along, a cockroach that blindly creeps. I am alone. . . . Where are thou, O my Sun? Help me. Do not cease to help me.

Everything I know about the world outside I know thanks to Giovanni, the jailer assigned to me, and due to the strange direction my life hath taken, the human being with whom I have the most genuine of friendships. Giovanni was born at the foot of Vesuvius, not far from this hill, in one of the many cottages from which it is possible to admire from a distance, and not without circumspection, the defensive walls that separate the quiet countryside from the teeming city of Naples. He is of good character, even though coarse and irascible. He hath become attached to me with affection, which comes in part from the deference of peasants to men of the cloth, in part from the orderliness and cleanliness of my cell, so different from the hovels of the other "tenants," as he calls them disparagingly. So every day, Giovanni arrives in front of my door in search of a brief respite, and protected by the wall that separates us, he opens up to me, shares insignificant confessions, recounts anecdotal morsels of the life outside this castle, about scuffles between his wife and his four sisters, about what he sees and feels when he goes out into the streets of Naples. We also partake of a small secret: probably my only joy as an inmate of these four walls. Speaking of this and that, Giovanni disclosed to me his curious predilection for the delicacies prepared in some Genoese inns, dishes that he discovered in the vicinity of a church that the merchants from the north dedicated to Saint George. What happens is that, thanks to a secret under-standing between him and the prison cook, each Friday, a certain Genoese recipe is prepared for the guards of Saint Elmo, and so every week on that day, the entire castle is per-meated with the aromas of beef, celery, and onion. For my companions in misfortune, this is a further punishment. For me, instead, these odors are an occasion for distraction. In fact, my mouth waters while I await the leftovers that I know Giovanni will smuggle out and throw into a cloth handkerchief. And I pray in the meantime for his soul, the gout that plagues his older sister, and a happy, lasting marriage between Lord Celery and Lady Onion.

Last night, I dreamed again of Leyla, or should I say the mother, this woman who in another millennium, far from these shores, will have the strength, the stubbornness, and the impudence to bring me once again into this world. I have seen her forced into a life of flight, of constant exile, if for no other outcome than the one generated in her womb out of my fluid; and yet, as far as I can tell, hers will be the flight of a woman besieged by herself. Over the course of several nights, in fact, I followed her while, having left the countryside of my birth-place, she strode discontentedly between crystal towers in a town ten times more extensive and more populated than ours and similarly populated by devilish contraptions and muskets of every type. And yet, during those dreams, I did not catch sight of the father with the Mayan face. Shouldn't I have been able to see him again at least once? And wouldn't he have known how to find us again in this grotto lost among the crystal citadels? I have been feeling that the magnetic force exerted on the mother by our old continent would have irremediably lost us. On the other hand, the tension that coursed through this woman—that of an arrow an instant before release—was identical to what I have been feeling myself in this cell. So, when I awoke, I could not help but wonder what was true and what was merely aspirational. What my oppressors never knew and still in fact do not know is that it was not the chains or the isolation that broke my resistance; it was because I myself lost hope and collapsed—a marathoner a foot from the finish line. Sometimes, one deludes oneself into thinking that the blindness of another can bolster the veracity of our science. Unfortunately, what we ourselves lack is mirrored by another's ignorance. I believed I was acting on behalf of what is right, but ultimately, I, too, was guilty of benign arrogance and vanity. I thought I had found the right way forward, one foot before the other, but was I really following the path of the Lord, our God? Too late I realized I was in error and that my anger was the hatred of the foolhardy man who accuses another when he is incapable of looking within himself. During the long months of darkness and silence in this cell, self-analysis becomes inevitable. And after having been visited by demons and having spoken with the angels, I learned that life after death is more than a dream: it is the certainty of the solitary. Enclosed within this mortal coil, like the butterfly in its cocoon, we are then tossed onto the stage of an upside-down world, where every role acquires a paradoxical meaning. Thus, if one is Socrates, the choice left is either flight or death, but if thy name is Nero, thou become the emperor, win the love of many, and then thou burn this multitude like twigs of wood. And so I write, and every phrase, every word consumes me. I defy fatigue, darkness, and inertia because, once the body becomes ash, it can, via the spirit, recover its correct symmetry. In the hope of everlasting memory, I leave these words of mine:

O thou, lifelike death, nest of ignorance,
Wearable sepulcher and vestment
Of guilt and torment,
The weight of worry and labyrinthine error,
Thou quash me with affectations and dread,
And prevent me from seeking my own abode
    in the heavens
And the good that comes before all other:
Hence, enchanted and overcome by its beauty
I do not despise and leave thee, lifeless ember.
(T.C. Settimontano Squilla)

Two Years Later

They were right to take advantage of my desire for freedom, but they were mistaken when they gave a meaning to that hope, a slight hint of one. My dreams are much more banal and simple: the dream, for instance that they might start reading my writings, the mirage that they may spread from Germany to our peninsula and, who knows, that there may even be someone understanding them, that one day they could reach all the way to the hands of the Holy Father. Of course, I long to find myself one day face-to-face with His Holiness Paul V, to see him nod in my presence; and after months of incessant requests, this dream of mine was on the verge of being realized. In fact, I had succeeded in being granted a joint audience with the Nuncio Aldobrandini and Diodato Gentile, the papal inquisitor. To obtain it, I had to plead, grovel, and feign suicidal intentions. Despite this, when they finally showed up in my cell, I sensed—and it was an almost-tactile sensation—the paltry nature of human ambition, the depth of a servitude that hath no need of a hovel such as my own to reveal itself. One would expect that being free to roam, raised in luxury, and exposed to the many arts and marvels produced either by genius or by mother nature, these two men of the Church would be able, in the cave of a wicked man, to alleviate his woes, if not with a ges-ture of comfort, at the very least with a tentative smile. However, when they arrived at my cell, they appeared as two sullen masks, two straw scarecrows. It would have been enough to have some sense of them, to catch their living and scornful eye, to feel their animal weight and size, their resistance not as it applies to the act of compassion but to its ideal. It would have been enough, I say, if their speech had not betrayed such inhuman indifference. I understood that

I was irreparably lost. Aldobrandini interrupted my supplications with a reprimand: "Campanella, thou lack humility, and humility is magnanimous, not cowardly, as thou seem to believe." Gentile reinforced the statement: "I fear that the time thou gave to sects and cults hath distracted thee from the true God." And after a derisive smirk, "I believe, my dear Campanella, that the only miracle that thou may attempt to perform is the one that will restore freedom to thee, but for that, it doth not take magic but sincere repentance."

After Another Year

A year after that bizarre encounter, I resolved to write a long missive to the Holy Father. I put it down on paper posthaste, without pretense and frills of any kind. I revisited my stumbling blocks, my misunderstandings. I revealed to him those diabolical meetings at the time of my first captivity at Castel Nuovo, hinting at the secrets whispered to me by Beelzebub and examining in detail the hundreds of saints and philosophers condemned for having uttered insights ahead of their time. Ultimately, I promised to be his right hand, to help him in the conversion of heretics, to champion him against the Venetian enemy, to perform all these and other wonders with the book that I am girding myself to finish. With this manuscript of mine, in fact, I am exposing Machiavelli's untruth, the political flaw that hampers human solidarity on its primordial path. With this book, I show the simplicity of our credo, the affinities between the adult age of the species and its first infancy. Via an excursus, which moves from Pythagorean, Stoic, and Epicurean philosophy, straight through to the lessons of Telesius, I delve into the secrets of all the ancient and modern sects, and I demonstrate the words of Christ found in Hebrew codices, as well as in Turkish, Persian, and Chinese ones. I reveal his teachings in the conduct of the Japanese, Brahmins, Peruvians, Mexicans, and Abyssinians. Will the Holy Father be able to admit that the law imposed on us by Christ is first and foremost a natural law, or will he find, in his turn, that Campanella hath lost his mind? And in that case, will his magnanimity be able to grant that forgiveness reserved for the tailor who manages to ruin many a cloth before the clothing is created, and for the doctor who manages to kill many an invalid on his way to becoming a worthy and skillful practitioner of his profession?

Naples, Kingdom of Naples—May 1607: Still at Castel Sant'Elmo

Haggard are those who, in solitude and secret, research my writings, recall the name of "he" who, in what already seems to be prehistory, was the revolutionary Tommaso Campanella. For many others, on the other hand, I was nothing but a shadow whose very existence is the subject of speculation and slander. I can count my friends on the fingers of one hand. Among the few remaining, I struggle to decide on whom to rely. From distant admirers, messages arrive—promises—but how many of these well-intentioned words of comfort and compassion have I seen dissolve into dust in the wake of a comet? It is for this reason that the arrival of the German, Kaspar Schoppe, in Naples assumed—and I realize only for me—the striking characteristics of a miracle. And even more so, when tireless, caring, and as beautiful as the Archangel Gabriel, he secretly slipped himself into my cell with the force of a lightning bolt. Holding my knees between his hands, he told me of the countless marvels he had witnessed in the viceroyalty of Naples. He also gave me a report of my following in the city and the continent, and I still feel a certain amount of difficulty in expressing the emotions generated in me by his description of the Caravaggio painting at the Pio Monte based on a horoscope Manso had asked of me years ago. In the words of Schoppe, the artist had transposed in images my natural religion but without surrendering its astrological trace: a Venus in the Virgin's clothing dominating and calming a tiny Mars or, in other words, Saint Martin. Then, without getting lost in pleasantries, he shared his eagerness to possess me like the goddess of love in that painting. He talked of the months spent in finding me, the shortcuts gleaned from friends and acquaintances to undermine the circle around his prey. In the end, driven by a feeling beyond all reason, he enumerated the actions he had undertaken for my liberation and—to my mind, more probably—for the publication of my writings. Other so-called friends and followers had approached me in the past in the guise of seraphim, but on these occasions, a quick exchange was enough to unmask the sham. This time, I feel it is different. Is Schoppe, then, just like the archangel? Doth he represent for me the fearless Samson? Is he a friend? A confidant? Could he be the true face of love?

The sky is full of stars and deep, deep like a stormy sea, deep like the recesses of a violent, unruly, voracious sea. Against the backdrop of turquoise blue, the stars sparkle intensely. They are diamonds smooth and polished by centuries of hope. Schoppe hath been successful where no one hath, and it doth not matter if it is a story of merely one night. It doth not matter if, at the crack of dawn, this adventure will have already assumed the contours of memory. "Tonight we go out," Giovanni said to me. Tommaso shouts and springs up. "This night is thine." I do not know how much exactly he was offered to buy his silence, what may have been the price for this brief exhilarating escape of mine, but I know that Giovanni would not have taken this risk for others, and I will have to come back here—no doubt about it. Having said this, this exit will extend my life a few more decades. The entire plan hath been agreed on and drawn up in detail: at sunset, there is a change of guard. Giovanni begins his shift, and Schoppe is behind him but remains down below; while waiting for the appointed time, Giovanni covers and monitors the entrances, and as soon as the time is right, he brings me to him. Even if someone saw us, no one would suspect Giovanni. It will be him, anyway, who, on my return at sunrise, will close this parenthesis of liberty with a double twist of the lock.

We moved away from the prison and we came to the square of the charterhouse. It was then that the sky opened up before us like a peacock's tail, and from out of that tide came the buried souls. Right away, we descended the Pedamentina stairway. We rushed toward the lower city, and having passed the Gravina Palace, we hid among the patrons of the Locanda del Cerriglio. We ate. We caroused. We tried to blend with them. We danced until we spied, a short distance away, a group at a bench and, in the middle of it, a drunken swordsman. Schoppe informed me it was Michelangelo Merisi da Caravaggio—the artist of *The Seven Works of Mercy*—and that, beyond the tough exterior, he was in the habit of being, at least with those who flattered him, affable and courteous. I knew I had to meet him. I made my way toward him, approaching him from behind, but with the reflexes of a warrior and despite his drunkenness, he swung around with a sudden jerk, clutched at my hood which I had let fall onto my neck, and seized me by the nape. Lifting up my hands in surrender, I explained to him that I was Tommaso Campanella, the friend of Manso and that his painting had been inspired by a horoscope of mine. I did not speak to him of our nocturnal escape. I preferred that he believe it was an actual release from prison. Did he know that his painting was inspired by one of my horoscopes? He immediately changed expression. His face broke into an enchantingly wide smile. His grip became an embrace. He asked me if I wished to see it in person; he had on him a key to the chapel. Then, not waiting for a reply, he exclaimed, "Come! I want thee to see it!" We entered the chapel warily and closed the main door behind us. Then, by candlelight, I moved deeper inside, while the artist, suddenly hesitant, lingered on the threshold. Moonlight slithered along the bare walls, and the flame created long and sinister moving shadows on the floor. Still hesitant, the artist pointed out a row of candelabras, accessible by a small ladder and capable of illuminating, once lit, the upper portions of the canvas he had painted. Kaspar whispered in my ear, "The flickering of light is probably due to the artist's tremors." Yet, from my viewpoint, engulfed in grace and no longer mindful of my prison life, I could not reproach Caravaggio. But as the flames of the candles gradually began to sputter and fizzle out, I felt a new kind of fire burning in my chest. What the artist had built for me towered over everything else like an everlasting legacy. Behold my Moon, disguised as an ancient Pero, and tied to her earthly master by mutual attraction! Behold Mars, as the elegant warrior in the guise of Saint Martin, albeit softened by a Venus of charity and love. Then there was Mercury, dressed like a pilgrim with the seashell on his hat, then jovial Jupiter, and beside these, Saturn as a colossal and merry Samson. And as if mirroring me, from the back of the painting a lay cleric sprang forward, carrying, like I was, a torch in his hands—the Sun, undoubtedly—fulcrum of this wonderfully simulated constellation, and nucleus of a round dance in which, since time immemorial, we have all been spinning. I turned toward Schoppe. I was ready to be led back to my cell. A rift had been opened in space and time. I understood that every defeat of mine had brought me to this night, as well as every injustice, every loss, because grief charts cracks in the cosmos, because through this artwork, I would touch the multitudes, years and centuries into the future. And so it mattered little that a few weeks from this night, both Schoppe and Caravaggio would leave Naples. The seed of freedom had definitely bloomed, as splendid as a sunrise that works its way through the mountains, as immense as my spirit, already permeating the spirit of others, in other centuries, continents, and forever nourished by their hopes.

～ 9 ～
Michael

He would take a direct flight from New York, JFK; then he would disappear into the alleyways of Naples as Caravaggio had, four hundred years before. After Leyla had kicked him out, Pablo had initially fallen back on their relationship, but he suffered constantly at the thought that his beloved and their son were inaccessible, although less than two miles away. So he asked Michael for a break. He said that he "had to sort his life out." Michael, for his part, had given up on Pablo the moment that Tommaso had come into the world. In the meantime, he had managed to finish his courses with excellent grades. He had majored in history of art and could not wait to see in person the many paintings that he had marveled at in the faded pages of art books and catalogs over the course of his studies. And then, since he was all alone, he could not see any reason for waiting around for the graduation ceremony. He knew it was not his lot to share in the general merriment, and he knew he would be much less convinced by the optimistic addresses of the invited guest speakers. "How can they possibly promise a future they know nothing about? And how will I be able to conceal my annoyance?" he wondered. What he feared most, however, was that staying on at the university would allow the feeling of alienation that had engulfed him for over three years to fester and intensify. He would be in the way, out of place, and since he himself didn't like the attention-seeking attitudes of killjoys, he decided that it was better to just leave and take himself as far away as possible. Besides, a fresh and springlike smile had recently resurfaced on his face for no apparent reason. It was one of those indecisive smiles that are often revealed to be the most sincere and enduring. He already could see the end of his last year of university, a year that had seemed long and bothersome like those interminable hospital hallways lit up twenty-four hours a day and populated by a thousand miserable faces. For a great while, it had seemed to him that he was going from door to door, corridor to corridor. Then, all of a sudden and as if by chance, he found himself at the labyrinth's exit. Leaving Saint Luke University marked the end of a journey. Everything was ready: he had cleared his own room of all personal effects, had thrown away anything that wasn't immediately useful, and gathered up all the rest to put into only two small suitcases. He was cheerful, feeling a bit cocky, pleased with his practicality, with what his French professor had once called his *esprit de synthèse*. He read his final essay a few times before handing it in, as if to postpone the agony, to punish himself, to better savor his rediscovered freedom. He wanted to show off his sense of responsibility, to verify that nothing had been rashly dealt with, like someone who, before throwing himself off the balcony, tidies the house, dusts the furniture, and makes sure that every single thing is nailed down where it will stay into eternity. He finally wrote his name at the top of the exam paper. He used bold capital letters. But he forgave himself right away for this bravado. He was getting ready to change his life, and why blame himself for wanting to inject a bit of daring into his existence? He handed in his paper, said goodbye to his professor—the best professors were always those teaching the last class—and hurried toward his car. He expected to get to New York within eight hours at the most—around four in the afternoon. He had already reached an agreement for the sale of his car on an online site and had an address in Brooklyn where he would be able to leave it. From there, he would call a taxi and head to JFK. His flight was scheduled for 9:00 P.M.

Naples, Italy—May 2010

When he tried to interpret the sensation he felt as soon as he got off the plane at Capodichino, what came to mind was one word: fear. He felt fear in the taxi that, at a snail's pace, took him to his hostel. He was afraid to say "si" when he knew not a single word of Italian. He nodded at anything suggested to him, and what if he was giving consent for the sale of his organs? All of a sudden, he was terrified of being alive. Once he arrived at the hostel, he became aware of an almost-paranoid terror with regard to the two Germans with whom he shared this room for extended accommodation and who, even though they spoke English, did not seem to be interested in him in the least. He was scared of fleas, of scabies, and of the transvestites standing at the corner of the street. And yet, despite this fear, having barely placed his luggage on the floor, he was out the door and on the street. Motor scooters whizzed by him. Hurrying passersby shoved him. An old man stopped him and asked a question and at the dazed, tongue-tied, and embarrassed answer from Michael, spit on the ground and continued walking. And yet somehow, he felt invincible, all the while knowing that they could rip him to pieces. There was an old Egyptian legend set in Naples that he read many years before. In it, the parts of a hacked-up body knew how to find and be magnetically pulled toward each other. Today, with the help of an old map, he easily found his way onto the street called Via Toledo. From there, he walked up to Piazza Plebiscito, carried by his legs and guided by an infallible sense of direction. He ate a *pizza rustica*, a savory pie that he had bought at a kiosk on the street, and as he pointed his finger at it, he wondered if it were possible to survive in Italy by virtue of a simple hand gesture. He then entered the National Library and—he did not know exactly how—filled out an entry form in Italian. He felt clever, enterprising, practical: in the space of a few hours, he had found a safe nesting place, and from that lair, he would begin his conquest of the city.

Naples, Italy—October 2010

In his first months in Naples, he wandered around like a stray animal, propelling himself toward the main tourist attractions. Nevertheless, during the summer, which he spent dividing his time between Capri and Ischia, he renewed his decision to use the autumn to penetrate further, although gradually, into the pounding heart of the city, to discover all of its nooks and crannies, visit every single church, even the humblest and forgotten, even the closed ones of which he was sure he could procure the keys from some hidden custodian. All in all, he had decided to adopt Naples. "Too bad," he admonished himself lightheartedly, "that Naples doesn't know it yet." He also realized that being a foreigner gave him extraordinary freedom to maneuver. Yet, he wanted his roaming to have purpose. He wanted to come into contact with what would have been the Naples of Tommaso Campanella and Caravaggio. He needed to establish a center, some criterion for urban exploration. After some research, he decided to begin from the intersection of the streets of Via Nilo and Via Benedetto Croce, where the neglected and misunderstood statue of Nile, the so-called Body of Naples, towered above everyone and everything. He told himself that even Tommaso Campanella would have started there, and so he, too, had to begin his journey at that crossroads. Where it would take him, however, he had no idea.

He woke up at dawn and used the first hours of the morning to shave, prepare, and organize the long day that was unfolding before him like the page of a papyrus manuscript. In front of the mirror, he thought about how every motion brings with it years of involuntary lifelong learning; he wondered if he would start to think about his grooming in a whole other way in Naples. Finally, he went out, still a bit unsure and with a terrible sensation of having forgotten something. A few minutes later, he was already in Piazzetta Nilo, standing before the eponymous statue erected there thousands of years ago in memory of the Egyptian sieges that had occurred around the third century A.D.—or at least that was what the Touring Club guidebook said. At first, he felt if not exactly disillusionment, something that was similar to a sense of melancholy. This monument, which Tommaso

Campanella would have admired in his first strolls through the city and then distractedly skirted around in his comings and goings to and from the Church of San Domenico, today appeared like a ruin, blackened by pollution and abandoned due to the neglect of its citizens. Some pieces of the statue seemed to be missing; others had been affixed only later on. Could this terrible example of bricolage mark the beginning and the end of his journey of initiation? He felt assailed by doubt. Continuing to observe the statue, however, his original uncertainty quickly gave way to sympathy. All things considered, was it fair to ask of a statue that had, after all, survived its battle with time in a dignified manner, to have also done it with pomp and circumstance, and then exclusively for him? From the Touring Club pages, it wasn't clear when the statue of the god of the Nile had lost its head and when they had added a different one. The body, at any rate, had evidently continued to live, as if animated by its own intelligence. Soon, this frowning god began to seem like a leathery and tough old man, a true miracle of grit and determination. Michael moved closer to it, and in that moment, he noticed the little cherub desperately climbing up the chest of the Nile god, searching for any nipple at hand to stick into his mouth. It was an odd sight. He said to himself, "I could never have hoped for a better beginning—an androgynous body without a head," and lost in thought, he pressed his hand against a turgid nipple of his own in the grip of a new sense of euphoria and a pleasurable state of excitability. For the first time after months and months, he felt ready to reflect on his previous life, the reasons that brought him to Naples: his father, Jackson, Pablo, a world that seemed all of a sudden extremely far away. When in the past, people had talked to him about destiny, he had rolled his eyes. And yet, there must have been something to it because when he returned to the hostel, he found a letter waiting for him on the bed. He opened it. "I have definitely given up the idea of winning back Leyla and my son. I have left the United States and I will join you very soon." It was a delectable lie, the most beautiful, the sweetest, the most heartbreaking of all.

He spent entire days wandering through the streets of the historic center. Pablo's letter had thrown his plans into disarray and confounded his itineraries. The entrance and exit of the labyrinth into which he had thrown himself seemed to confuse him. He looked at his last years as one would at a cinematographic montage and he was no longer sure of the order of the frames. What he did know for sure was that independently of how many times a day he revisited those backstreets, he inevitably ended up coming back to the point of departure. One afternoon, having arrived at the Via dei Tribunali, he stopped at the Church of Santa Maria della Pace to get some rest. He was curious to check out the inside because during one of his haphazard searches at the National Library, he had read about the story of sin and redemption associated with this minor church, of the evils that it had generated, of the iniquities that it had harbored, of the sins that due to the upheaval caused by extraordinary events had been atoned for in this same church. In fact, the stately palace, which only later would become a religious institution, had served as a backdrop to the turbulent tale of love and adultery between Maria d'Avalos and Fabrizio Carafa. But this place did not plunge into scandal in vain, nor did it do so without the fact that redemption—if redemption actually existed—turned out to be the end of its unfortunate protagonists. Being caught in flagrante delicto by the Prince of

Venosa, husband of the lady, the two lovers were murdered in cold blood in the very same chamber that had witnessed their sexual passion. A short time later, these rooms were shut down. The chapel of the Lazzaretto would then be built right over the ashes of the unfortunate lovers, and from that structure, this church of Santa Maria della Pace grew like a symbol of triumph over death. Entering the church through a side door, Michael could still appreciate the suffocating space, which for decades had housed the victims of the plague, as well as the balcony from which the doctors, servants, and a new generation of zealous scientists dropped food and ointments for the invalids, with a technique of ropes and baskets, still being used in all the side streets of Naples. Michael thought about his own affairs, about the adultery in which he had participated, about the series of interruptions and rebirths that his exodus from the United States had triggered. But as in the case of the unfortunate Maria d'Avalos, he knew well that the roots of sin, though deeply buried, always found a way to reach the light of day, piercing through the gravel of centuries, to the point of breaking through cement floors. He left the church, still saturated by the sickly exhalations of those sixteenth-century plague sufferers. He felt as if he were suffocating. Once outside on the Via dei Tribunali, he began to walk aimlessly since, in that moment, he only wanted to get away from what felt like a trap. So he walked up the little known Via Pietro Trinchera, which was once a noble boulevard. He ended up in the open space in front of the Church of Santi Apostoli, beside a large building that a rusty sign let him know was a secondary school of the arts. He pulled his Touring guide out of his backpack and read that today's classrooms in the school had been the ancient residence of the Theatine priests of

Naples and thus the last home of the poet Giambattista Marino, Campanella's great friend. The author of the guide-book added, "Built on the spot where the Temple of Mercury once stood, the church was one of the four basilicas of Paleo-Christian Naples." He decided to go inside, and once there, he immediately noticed how the glow of the frescoes and the spiral-shaped choruses of the angels did not have anything of the tenebrist style introduced into Naples by Caravaggio. He concluded that it was probably for this reason that no one had ever spoken much about this church. Nonetheless, what caught his attention more than the jubilance of colors up there on the vaulting was the extensive fresco that loomed over the entryway and in particular the angel, an updated Mercury representing the new credo, one that transformed with a wave of a magic wand the lepers' pool into a probatic pool. So he pulled out Pablo's letter from the lining of his overcoat and mused that this poor letter could be anything, that all that would be necessary was to conceal it, convert it, transform it with a wave of a magic wand. If Mercury could do it, so could he.

At first, he had felt like a castaway adrift at sea. Despondent and fearful, Pablo had faced a day and a night of travel without knowing what to expect. He was terrified at the prospect of not finding Michael, of failing once again, and this time, of having to withstand that failure—he had laughed at this expression, "a failure of global importance." In the meantime, Michael remembered the letter that he had dismissed in a sudden surge of irritation and that he nonetheless safeguarded in the lining of his coat like a promise. And so, in spite of himself, he couldn't repress a sly look of joyous apprehension before this ghost with a clay face, this out-of-context mask of regret, like a Christmas gift offered in August. In that precise instant, he understood that every gesture, every decision, every ultimatum lay in his hands, from this time forward. Thus, while Pablo continued to look at him with exhaustion from too many nights of insomnia, Michael couldn't find anything better to say than "How are you? What are you doing here in Naples?" To which Pablo answered by suddenly bursting into tears, though so briefly, that it seemed like nothing more than a single sob; after that, having wiped his eyes with the back of his hand, he shaped his lips into a blithe smile and woodenly threw himself into Michael's arms, not knowing what else to do. Michael felt the same annoyance that Leyla must have, the revulsion felt toward someone who, in giving himself completely, subtly enslaves you. But he also experienced enormous tenderness and an almost-religious call that he had sensed vis-à-vis Pablo from their first encounter. Fighting against his survival instinct, he put an arm around Pablo's shoulders, and in this position—a rather uncomfortable one—he guided him speedily toward the hostel where he was still living, protecting him from the world's gaze, from his very own fears, and from the various demons that they both hid within themselves. It was 3:00 in the afternoon when they arrived.

"It was stupid of me not to follow you immediately. I mean . . . I was the stupid one," said Pablo.

"Maybe it was stupid to come and look for me here. It would have been unfair to ask you to do it. . . . And, by the way," Michael responded, chuckling, to provoke him a bit, "who invited you?"

Pablo put a hand on his mouth but only lightly touching it. They craved closeness, silence, and the time necessary for a long-awaited but perhaps impossible healing.

Around Six Months Later

Pablo became integrated into the city with a staggering rapidity, and Michael couldn't help but feel slightly envious. For months, he had tried to communicate in Italian, resorting to phrase books of every kind, laboriously memorizing the various sentences, which when necessary, escaped him. Pablo, instead, had begun to speak Italian in his own bastardized and creative version from the moment he had set foot in Naples, histrionically making use of phrases learned from old neorealist films or by falling back on Spanish any time he was at a loss for words. Thanks also to that natural sociability of his, which in the States was often mistaken for bravado, he could strike up a conversation with the downtown shopkeepers and launched into improvisations that left Michael astounded and forced other people to follow Pablo around, the way wild cats shadowed each other in any Mediterranean medina. In short, after less than two weeks since his settling into the hostel, Pablo could already count more friends and acquaintances than what Michael had managed to make since his arrival in this city and actually more than he had ever had. It was as if the new life that he had dreamed of on his departure from the States had been torn from his hands by the friend and companion who was supposed to actually complement it—as if, in a struggle for survival of which no one had deigned to inform him, Pablo had proven himself to be more ambitious, more competitive, and just better at it. On the other hand, it was at his side that he was able to see in Pablo an avidity, an insatiable desire to live that plunged the latter—at times even dangerously—into blind desperation. More than once, faced with the noisy impetuousness and indiscretion of his new Neapolitan companions, Pablo had felt himself driven to do worse. Michael had to berate him, and not infrequently, for his excesses in alcohol consumption and more and more often for his habitual disappearances. When they were in Saranac Lake, Michael had loved Pablo's totally inclusive generosity, his utter lack of affectation or mannerisms, his shameless authenticity. However, this desire to please everyone at all costs had transformed him here in Naples into a crass loudmouth. Michael could barely tolerate him. Sometimes he would have liked to write to Leyla to apologize, to tell her that she had been right, that he had understood too late. Unfortunately, he realized that his professor of old had no need of any kind of corroboration, and he shamefully felt that his admiration for her belonged unequivocally to that category of love, which homosexuals of every age cultivate in solitude, by clinging to a word or a smile from the muse of the moment, as one would hang on to the raft of the Medusa.

Then, conversely, there were days he felt that with Pablo by his side, he had penetrated the tactile universe of happiness. The walks during which they discovered churches and monuments were no longer journeys of the imagination but concrete experiences, memories to share. It was a warm day at the end of winter when they climbed the Pedamentina stairs toward Largo San Martino. Once there, they looked at the city that extended below them, just as Campanella could have done five hundred years before from his prison in Castel Sant'Elmo. Up until that day, Michael had never pushed himself all the way to the Certosa monastery. He had never gone inside. In his first weeks in Naples, he had postponed the visit more than once. Then that, too, went into the annals of those activities to put off for another time—namely, the ones he never managed to do. Now that he finally had the opportunity to visit it, he told himself that this deferral was no different than what is hidden behind every failure; even the cause of this one, in the end, had been romantic anticipation.

When they entered the courtyard of the Certosa, Michael had an immediate impression of safety. Far from the world and as if projected into another dimension, he wondered what living in constant silence must have meant for those cloistered monks, prisoners of themselves, as of their cells. Pablo asked him, somewhat mischievously, if he thought that once in a while those monks cheated by softly whispering a word to each other, but he abstained from sharing any further thoughts, fearful of disappointing Michael again. From the entry forecourt, they headed toward a second cloister, where long garlands of skulls decorated the balustrade that encircled the garden of orange trees. They had thus spent around a half hour in the church of the Certosa only to realize, once outside, that it was possible to visit sections beyond the walls of the building, along a sequence of corridors that made them lose their concentration. Michael sighed: "A little like life, we have here a chain of rooms, where the first are the most interesting or, who knows, the only ones to which we are prepared to pay attention." However, there was an anecdote about the church that Michael wanted to share before they left. In his opinion, it was that kind of story that, whether true or not, brought life to a historic era. This anecdote stemmed from the competition between two baroque painters, Ribera and Stanzione—a Spaniard and a Neapolitan—both engaged by the Carthusian fathers to paint a Pietà, both young and ambitious. According to the version known by Michael, Ribera, envious of his rival, somehow infiltrated the church at night and, in the dark, defaced Stanzione's painting. "But Stanzione," continued

Michael, "wasn't upset." In fact, not only did the malevolence of the most famous Spanish painter confirm his own talent—a talent he still doubted—but it seemed to him that the damage done to his work humanized his Christ at the foot of the cross. Still today, in the twenty-first century, the two Pietà paintings remained in the church as a reminder of a rivalry that had seen both artists win the contest over time. That of Ribera loomed, dismal and funereal, over the end of the treasure hall; that of Stanzione, instead, remained on the wall opposite the altar and therefore above the front portal, with the same humility, discretion, and tenderness of its shrewd craftsman. For reasons that in that moment he deemed unfathomable, Michael found himself wondering for which of the two images of Christ Pablo could pose and function as model. But it was a useless question and, all things considered, a rhetorical one as well. Pablo would never have accepted to relegate himself to the lunette of a counter altar, much less allow time and light to alter his facial characteristics. Just like the statuary and on par with the helpless and damaged Christ by Ribera, Pablo, heroic and theatrical, was incapable of playing any role other than that of protagonist.

Naples, Italy—June 2011

It was a warm morning. The aroma of pastry cream wafted through the windows, blending in rather violently with the sewage fumes, the exhaust from motor scooters, and the vibrant, perturbing, and pungent odor of the oleanders. Michael, as usual, got up before everyone—that is, before the German tourists snoring like wild boars, in spite of their reputation of efficiency and punctuality; before Pablo, impervious to light and noise; before the staff, tasked with preparing the breakfasts and who were, as it happened, punctually late. He left the room barefoot, carefully placing his feet on the cold terracotta and trying not to make noise. To while away the time, he then decided to take along his Touring Club guidebook—a guidebook that had been an inseparable companion to Campanella's biography over the course of his first year in Naples and that he had to find among the pile of novels read and thrown aside. When he finally did, he saw that its cover was creased and crushed and rebuked himself for his carelessness. While looking through the pages, he lingered on the passages highlighted during his first weeks in Naples, the ones about the places and works that he had wanted to visit but never did. In fact, he was turning those pages, somehow discomfited by how little he had been able to see and study, when he felt unexpectedly vexed and nauseated, sensations, that—originally attributed to the mixture of odors spilling into the room in gusts—quickly resulted in a hazy realization. He had consciously chosen to be transported by instinct and by the labyrinthine streets of the city, maybe to imitate the early twentieth-century flaneurs—but the Pio Monte della Misericordia, with Caravaggio's *Seven Acts*, was the only place, the only destination that he did not want to miss. So what had happened? How weak he must have been to make himself be distracted to such a degree. He felt a strong desire to cry, to chastise himself. Then, perhaps because of the prevalence of the custard-like smell over all the others, he told himself that there was a remedy to everything: first, to his hunger, for which the noise of cups and cutlery coming from the dining room could represent an immediate answer, and second, to the gap in his knowledge, for which there existed "the key to everything." While one of the two Germans passed him with the bad-tempered air of having been woken too soon, Michael wondered if it was worth waiting for Pablo or if it might be better to head for the Pio Monte by himself.

He walked along Via dei Tribunali. This morning would belong exclusively to him. He had put off his goals for too long, procrastinated until he had betrayed his very own plans. He had shared everything with Pablo, and now he would save this painting by Caravaggio for himself alone. How beautiful and calm Naples was at this moment; how different it was to see the blue sky above the copestones of the buildings and then reflected in the puddles, the pastel-colored palaces, although marred and blackened, without the misery of screaming voices, without the brute faces of their inhabitants. Past Via Duomo, however, the street grew dark and sinister, and so Michael ran until he could slip through the huge iron fencing at the entrance to the Pio Monte. Then, thanks to the fortuitous absence of the security guard, he dashed into the interior of the chapel. Once inside, the painting appeared before him like an ancient mastodon, high and mighty and seemingly displeased for having been made to wait so long. It was almost impossible, because of the reflections on the varnish and the dark entry points, to get a unified vision of the work. Driven to look from the bottom of the canvas, Michael began to gaze at the image of Pero, the woman nourishing her chained and imprisoned father, and noticed maybe for the first time the small crown of fabric that she was wearing like a sliver of the moon. From her breast, spilling forth somewhat vulgarly, he passed on to the scene behind, where a toothless man, in shirt and beret, wielded a long torch, and accompanied a funeral procession with shouts and prayers. A corpse, whose feet were the only body part visible, was wrapped up and dragged in a sheet. He had been readily pushed off a bed, who knows whether to ward off pestilential emanations or to erase the traces of a carnal crime. In the upper part of the painting, the Virgin (of Mercy or the Nursing Madonna: neither he nor Leyla had been able to reach a definite conclusion) floated above the circle of twirling angels, and beneath them—and here, Michael was obliged to come and go continuously to focus on the image beyond the clash of colors—an improvised commotion: Samson with a bone remnant used as a water flask, an innkeeper who, rotund and ruddy, pointed to the closest lodging, and on the ground, one of the many desperate vagrants whom a local squire would rescue and exploit, proving that nothing much had changed since Caravaggio's time. He remembered having discussed the astrological beliefs of those years and the possible juxtaposition between the Virgin and the celestial Venus with Leyla. It was only in front of the painting, however, that he wondered if the *Seven Works* could not represent the seven days of the week or the house of the Sun and the planets gravitating around it. He observed that the warrior saint—Saint Martin, that is Mars—obscured another figure who could easily have functioned as Mercury, with the special headgear often associated with the celestial messenger. But when squinting, he wondered about that sneaky attitude, about that brim fallen down his face; he seemed like a fugitive. And so Michael asked himself why did Caravaggio and Campanella flee; why was everyone running away? He himself was running away. Leyla had run away. Those who ran away were maybe the ones who felt the world was squeezing them too tightly, was crushing them. What pain, what inner agitation, what turmoil was responsible? He surmised: it is nothing but a question of weight—one weight after another—a collapse, impossible to foresee, to predict even within a second of its occurrence—unstoppable—and along with this collapse, a fusion with the world, with the weight of the cosmos, the reverberation of other explosions, in that precise instant but light years away.

It was three days since Pablo had disappeared. He had left his bag and his personal belongings in the room. He was still in Naples, then. But where exactly? If it were any other person to vanish into thin air—a friend, an acquaintance— Michael would have been worried. However, in the case of Pablo, he did not feel apprehension but rather a searing pain in his side, a desperate anger, which after twenty-four hours had turned into something about to erupt. He was certain that Pablo had been approached by a series of middle-aged men, horny old men, who, in exchange for companionship, had lured him with luxuries and gifts, employing the dexterous alacrity of street vendors. They would be rich merchants exhausted by routine dullness, he, the eternal child who had never stopped searching for his father. Michael had not been able to protect him, but he found it hard to blame himself for this. He had let him be free, in Naples like at Saint Luke's, because he had learned that it was impossible to save someone who couldn't do it himself, because it would be better for everyone: better for Pablo, in fact, who, although surreptitiously, would be satisfying an atavistic desire; not terrible for the old lecher, who, thanks to Pablo's whim, would enjoy a final springtime, and certainly better for himself. He made up stories and rationalized to calm himself. And then he would experience a new surge of bile, of deep hatred. It would climb up his back, as if making use of a network of veins, a network already accustomed to a life of disappointment. He could no longer take this role of wingman. His father, Jackson, Pablo—everyone had abandoned him running toward something worse and depraved, throwing themselves headfirst into mud and leaving him behind spattered with the sludge, but he always remained understanding and forgiving. They were weak and messed up. But how much loneliness there was in this useless strength of his, how much silence. He told himself that for once, he could let himself be irresponsible. After all, Pablo was probably rolling around beneath the sheets in some villa in Posillipo, his father was getting drunk with his umpteenth travel companion, and the world kept on turning, indifferent to his stoic tolerance. So he picked up a pair of scissors and, without giving it a second thought, cut up the jeans he was wearing right up to his buttocks. Then he shaved his entire body. When he got down to the hairless skin of his childhood, he covered himself with cream and perfume and put on the tightest jersey he had. He headed like this, half adolescent boy, half slut, toward the basement of a building in Via delle Zite; he had already been to the underground locale in the past in search of a quickie, and he knew that things often got pretty degenerate. He had decided even before he stepped in that he would not reject anyone, that he would let himself be taken by the most decisive first-comer, by someone who was really serious about wanting him. The first man who approached him was of indefinable age, someone who drugs and pharmaceuticals had reduced to a stack of bones. The man seemed shy, perhaps aware of aiming too high, or maybe it was just a particular facial expression. And yet, it was precisely that reticence, that sick desire accompanied by a polite smile to convince Michael to approach him. He began by kissing his face, as he had done with his grandfather before he died. Then the man's mouth grew bold and going from the face to the back took a matter of seconds. The fact that he was working on him from behind with such alacrity, leaving him naked to the mercy of everyone, seemed to be no coincidence to the more brazen clients. He saw them coming over one at a time, like hyenas, while he was immobilized by his jeans pulled down to his ankles in a well-studied pose of sacrificial victim. In the beginning, he tried to count them, to quieten them down, and then he began to get confused, to lose count. He abandoned himself to the pleasure, to the pain, to what had to take place. He had never trusted anyone much in his life, nor had he ever truly given himself up to others. He woke up in the bed of a couple of professionals—lawyers, he told himself—who, in order to save him, had dragged him home, even though in their turn, they could not resist temptation and ended up continuing to overtax a body in which every sensation was like a faint electrical shock. While the two men were still asleep, Michael took a shower. He dressed in the dark, then headed toward the hostel. He felt proud, contented, only vaguely remorseful. When he arrived, he found the proprietor and a police commander in his room. They were rummaging through his and Pablo's things. Pablo was dead. His corpse had been found the afternoon of the day before, but it had been difficult to piece together the identity without documents. The body was extremely bloated. It lay in the back of a warehouse at the docks. The autopsy had established that death had taken place at least forty-eight hours before the discovery of the body.

PART 4

Thomas Eakins, *Amelia Van Buren*, ca. 1880s.

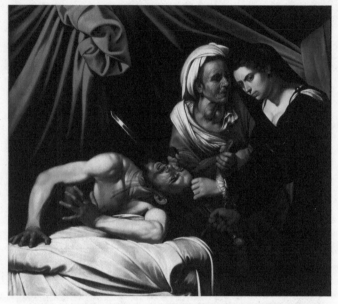

Louis Finson or Caravaggio, *Judith Beheading Holofernes*, 1610.

~ 10 ~

Michael

Paris, France—May 2019

His last months in Italy had been impossible, hellish. It was almost eight years ago that he had left Naples and, along with the city, that juncture in his life. And yet, every now and then, he still thought about it. Suddenly, his mind would return to those days full of anguish when images of the lifeless face of Pablo would appear to him as he glanced by chance at the greenish mildew on the pediments of buildings. The colors in these images blurred the contour lines, like in some expressionist portrait. In fact, once Pablo had died, the spell had been broken. The city had lost any and all romanticism. It no longer held any interest for him. America, on the other hand, was so far away, unwelcoming, unreachable. He wasn't the same. Life had irrevocably changed him. Then, in an afternoon of August 2011, a crystal-clear and sudden idea struck him: "It's time to leave." And although there had been no immediate follow-through to that thought, a week later, he had picked up his two small bags, thrown away everything except for some items of clothing he had a particular affection for—a pair of pants and two worn-out T-shirts was all he needed—and had quickly headed toward Naples Central Station. He was leaving Italy, in part because it was there that he had lost the gentlest and most vigorous piece of himself, in part to escape the morbid curiosity of the investigators who, although exonerating him, continued to summon him to their headquarters, regularly submitting him to interrogations that were as useless as they were obscene. From Naples, he had taken a fast train for Milan and, from there, a sleeper to Paris. He did not know if he would stay in Paris a month or a year. He could hardly have imagined that he would not leave the French capital ever again.

He had a microscopic studio apartment in the Marais, on Rue de Turenne, a job at the British Council, which occupied him from morning to night, and his constant companion was a deep depression. It never seemed to abandon him. Every evening, when he returned from work to this cramped room, he double-locked his front door, took off his jacket and shoes, and fully dressed, retired to his bed, which was separated from the window on the one side and the entrance on the other by two steps, of thirty, forty centimeters at most. In that position, he spent an infinite number of hours observing the cracks in the ceiling and, for the last few weeks, mentally contrasting them with the minuscule tears observed in the canvas of *Judith and Holofernes* in the Kamel Mennour Gallery, with the caption "Caravaggio" underneath it.

Squinting to better visualize them, he then compared those little fissures to the ones observed many times in the *Death of the Virgin* in the Louvre. "Was it the trademark of the artist's workshop?" he asked himself. "Could a crack be enough to identify an artist, the nervous weakness that spreads from the soul to the hand?" Every now and then, he thought of his mother, she, too, stretched out on a bed, her face looking up toward the ceiling, perhaps with her throat slit by an intruder or maybe simply drowned like the Madonna in the Louvre. The cracking of the plaster assumed the outline of arteries, varicose veins, channels, branches of blood broken by the fierce winds of life. He stayed on his back like this, sometimes for hours, until sleep conquered fatigue. Other times, instead, he jumped off the bed and mechanically headed for the kitchen stove. Lethargic and half-asleep, he made himself something to eat; almost always, he made do with a soft-boiled egg and a tuna salad.

He wandered around cafés, museums, and libraries and rarely was able to write for more than an hour at a time. Sometimes, before some painting or other, he regretted having stopped his studies in art history. He remembered Leyla's petulant voice. During his university years, she had kept on insisting that he should consider doing a doctorate, but she used arguments that, at the time of his first encounters with Pablo, he had relegated to background noise. Just this week, he had entered the church of Saint-François-Xavier on a whim, after walking through Saint-Germain, and there he had stumbled upon the *Miracle of the Crab* by Benedetto Gennari, a painting, in his opinion, much more worthy than Tintoretto's *Last Supper* that tourist guides cited as the only work of prominence in that church. Had he become the art critic that Leyla had hoped he would, he might have written about the glowing modernity of the Gennari's painting, and not so much because of the graphic feature of the waves or the phosphorescence of the pastel blue but for the shrewd pictorial conception by which the artist had turned the crab into the protagonist of the visual narrative—the obscene protagonist. It seemed to him, in fact, that the crucifix held firmly between the crab's claws and presented in this way to Saint Francis Xavier resembled a tumescent and disproportionately sized penis. Never had an "ecce homo" appeared so revealing to Michael, and certainly never before this day had the lemniscate curve, tying the body of the father to that of the son, assumed a configuration as unambiguous as it was naive. Still, Michael wavered. Was it right to bring an artistic interpretation back to one's own personal sensibility? All in all, he concluded, writing an autobiography would not be so different than writing about art; at the very least, he told himself, it could be a little less honest, a little more personal.

A Month Later

This was that period of the year in which, punctually, as in the previous eight years, his landlord brought him, with two months' notice, the lease renewal form, bowing and scraping and repeating that he would be truly happy if he stayed, that he couldn't hope for a better tenant, and that he "reluctantly" was forced to increase the rent because of inflation and the growing reputation of the neighborhood, "as you yourself must have noticed." The rental increase was minimal, he highlighted, and there wasn't any hurry at all to sign, except that he would be coming back regularly after exactly two months in an unfortunate cacophony of "Is this a bad time? Would you mind if I came in?" which suddenly stopped once he obtained the signed contract. In actual fact, despite a certain repugnance with regard to the landlord's arrogance and small-mindedness, the apartment on the Rue de Turenne had become a second skin for Michael, and what is more important, he neither had the strength nor the will to look for something better. He had found it, in fact, a short time after arriving in Paris and had been living there for years as if it were a lair, a cocoon, a mother's womb. She, however, his actual mother, he had not heard from in ten years. In the beginning, during his happy period in Naples, he hadn't written to her, in part because he was hell-bent on living, in part because of his difficulty in finding the right words. How was he going to tell her about Pablo? Where should he have started? At any rate, he kept promising himself that he would write to her a bit later, but the days and months flew by. In the meantime, Pablo had died, and he had gone through a whirlwind of emotions, the domino effect of the events, so that eventually, a sense of guilt had overtaken his self-indulgence. Living in a kind of trance, he could not think of writing an ever-longer but less-in-depth letter, one in which his excuses, which might have been convincing years before, would have gradually become meaningless. Ultimately, lethargy replaced his anxiety, and as his mother began to recede from his memory, she took on the consistency of a prayer card, an abstraction. What remained of her today, of her function between uterine and decorative, was nothing more than these four walls engaged in protecting him and circumscribing his world. He was free of every obligation. He could indulge every whim or indolence, but there were days when he wondered if this, too, might be a form, perhaps more surreptitious, of slavery and dejection. Besides, if only his landlord had an inkling of his attachment to this decrepit den, the monetary "inflation" in which his mouth seemed to revel, would surely have reached astronomical heights. Nevertheless, Michael pondered, beneath his apartment there was always Le Moulin de Rosa, and as to justify his inertia, he recognized that although Paris was not exactly lacking in boulangeries and pâtisseries, one need not take for granted the advantage of having one and, moreover, one of the best right downstairs, especially if one had an indolent nature to begin with. The gourmand awakening, guaranteed daily by the scent of croissants and the voices of the first customers, had for years lulled him into the illusion of being part of a close-knit community. And that Merwan Benyacar, a Jew of Turkish origins and manager of the Moulin, had immediately behaved like a long-established uncle of his, contributed more than a little to this false sense of security. Every morning, in fact, Merwan put aside a *pain au chocolat* for him, and when Michael finally came down from his apartment—between 7:15 and 7:30 A.M. at the latest—he could therefore count on a coffee and croissant, a friendly face, and a short chat with which to begin his day on a pleasant note. It would have been a bit much to declare that in Paris he had remade his life anew, but he could say without compunction that he had found in Merwan and in the man's daughter something that at least in a vague sense resembled a family.

Since he was little, he had hoped to achieve absolute peace, the least amount of movement. Instead, he had been sucked into the whirlpool of tragedy, the inconvenience of drama. He had tried to extricate himself, convinced that time would dissolve the sinister aura that the death of a lover casts on you. And yet, after years, he still bore the signs of those events, like those peasant women who bore a fuzz of facial hair, subtle but irrepressible. Making a pastime into a profession, during the months immediately following the discovery of

Pablo's body, he had made ends meet by working as a tour guide to groups of foreigners, but there were too many places in Naples at which he could not linger, too many monuments, which, assailed by memories, he pointed to from a distance. "Why would an American live in Italy? Why can't you take us to see that church? The *Routard* says it is a must-see." Observations like that on the part of tourists were enough to conjure up Pablo's ghost. Like it or not, as long as he stayed in Naples, he would remain nailed to a cross. Before his departure, however, he had had a funny and illuminating conversation with the police superintendent whom he had gotten to know over the course of the investigations surrounding Pablo's death. That morning, he was walking toward Port'Alba, having succeeded the evening before in convincing a bookseller to buy the over eighty guidebooks of the city that he had collected with maniacal persistence and that once in Paris, he would bitterly regret having sold. Overtaken by a sudden sociability and perhaps wishing to make official his decision to move to Paris, Michael had shouted to the superintendent on the opposite side of the street, "You know, sir, I am leaving for Paris!" "Finally," the man responded, as if not at all surprised, adding, "No foreigner should stay in this city for longer than a week. And most especially you, Mr. Michael, with all that has happened to you. In Paris, you will find a nice grouchy boyfriend and will spend your days in one of those cafés of Montparnasse where bohemians like you are meant to be. Then you can write about all that you have experienced here. It would make a nice book. Even Domenico Rea, one of our local writers has said so. . . . You live life or you tell it. And you, Mr. Michael, have lived it. Now go tell it." That was how—and he couldn't tell whether he had been driven by the memory of that conversation or by a deeper instinct—Michael had effectively begun to write a book. And despite this, so he thought, he had done it in hopes that he could reinvent his existence, cleanse it a little there where the outsized egos of the other actors had not allowed him to do it in the past. A sigh escaped him as he pondered: in this new universe of his, made up of characters more successful than the real ones, he would no longer be alone, "as if by magic." Suddenly, he began to chuckle in the midst of tears. "As if by magic," he ruminated, amused. He was thinking like a seventeenth-century man. He was thinking like Tommaso Campanella.

~ 11 ~

Tommaso Campanella

Paris, France—January 1635

I had continued to revise *Atheism Conquered*, attempting to respond, in the best way possible, to the criticisms— sometimes frivolous, sometimes accurate—of censors and adversaries. What bothered them most were my opinions on Machiavellianism, the suspicion that I was talking about them. They would never admit this, however, since it is easier to dredge up minutiae and doctrinal points than to see themselves reflected in the silver mirror of a guinea. Sometimes they halted accusations in the making. They appeared perplexed. They did not know if, when challenging my reading of the Gospel, they themselves were risking the stain of impiety, of heresy. So they tried to test me. They cited the Church Fathers, but they promptly went astray in theories that they had not mastered or that they could not debate. How to explain, for example, that the Mayans, an ancient civilization and so distant from us, celebrated confession and the Eucharist thousands of years before the Spanish conquest of the Americas, or that the imperturbable faith of the Ana-baptists had contained by itself the expansionists' ambitions of the Catholic Imperial Army? The religion that they believed bloomed solely in enclosed gardens spreads like weeds in every corner, and this is a realization that inevitably unnerves them. Since I have practiced free love, they accuse me of lewdness and debauchery. For having preferred the works of mercy to the passive action of Grace, they ascribe Pelagianism to me. And Cardinal Maffeo, who up until yesterday requested from me prophecies and astrological readings, resorted—when in the more rigorous robes of Urban VIII—to a thousand cautions and precautions. Thus, the friend who the day before was asking that the stars be manipulated in his favor, the day after launched a rather pernicious bull against any mingling with the stars. The result: Campanella was forced to make new revisions to his *Atheism Conquered*, the book was seized at the printer's, and once again, everything was sent back to the starting block. The pope challenged the book because he feared the author. And yet I convinced myself that with every new censure, with every new revision, my manuscript would emerge stronger than ever. Oh, how much grandiloquence to obfuscate fears and weaknesses! As if I had chosen it. As if the Lord Our God had not already preordained everything. As if my hand had not already been forced a long time ago.

A horse and carriage sent forth at a gallop in the middle of the night, a farcical disguise, a felucca incapable of sustaining the waves, the pressure of water getting the better of the wooden planks. All the nuances of mystery, of adventure, of sedition intensify the story of my escape into France, but it was not a glorious theatrical exit as much as it was a new point of departure that I would have gladly avoided. Regrettably, the news of Pignatelli's conviction did not leave any choice. I felt the itch on my neck. I saw the shadow of my condemnation spread around me. I knew it was time to flee the Roman swamp. With my youth dissipated between the walls of a cell, my old bones simply could not withstand any new agonies. For years, I had shouted from a black hole but in vain: one day, then a month, and finally light found an opening between the bars. The friendship of Urban VIII, his recognition, if not of my knowledge, then at least of my inclination toward good had finally prevailed. The pope in person had requested Campanella's liberation, but what followed on the heels of the pontiff's friendship was new slander, new jealousies, and only at the end the unhoped-for and glorious freedom, the sun that fortifies, restores, and rewards. It was 1629 when I was fully absolved, but my foot had not even covered the distance from the threshold of the prison to the arena of the world, and lo and behold, the vultures sharpened their sights, smelled my open wounds, and from the heights of their cardinal ranks, pounced on their prey, stabbing and ruthlessly bludgeoning their target. For months, prophecies of unknown origin had been circulating around Rome. They predicted the imminent death of the Holy Father, and he, who in public did not hesitate to denounce superstitions and beliefs, in the secrecy of his apartments remembered his friend Campanella, his ability to play with the stars and correct the bleakest of fates. If he is still alive— and he knows this well—it is all due to me. Together, we had tested the efficacy of those practices addressed in my opuscule, *De siderali fato vitando*. We had lit rosewood, cypress, and blueberry wood to disperse any and all poisonous influences. We had drawn magic circles, which protected him from the inauspicious influences of the stars, and made it so that these influences might be remedied and expelled. Having then closed all the shutters, we had equipped ourselves with two candles and five torches to imitate with these the sun, the moon, and the planets. And despite this, when every operation we carried out exclusively for the benefit of the church was made public by "an insidious friar," then we had to again justify ourselves, explain, rectify, while the Holy Father—now safe and comforted—was forced to distance himself from what the official directive dismissed as heretical superstition. To the accusations of judiciary astrology were then added those of conspiracy against Spain, and the memories of my lengthy incarceration bestirred me like dancing maenads. Only fools, in fact, do not recognize imminent danger. Thus, huddling in my damasked carriage, I fled toward the border, with the blessing of the Holy Father and a safe-conduct pass obtained from Du Plessis, the ambassador of the two Louis. And here I am in France, embracing the new life that Our Lord hath granted me, a life that will be more enduring, serene, and glorious than I myself could have ever hoped for.

A Year Later

Atheism Conquered finally saw the light of day in France.

~ 12 ~

Leyla

The contract in the Metropolitan Museum archives ended at the onset of the summer of 2011 for an apparent lack of funds, but the months she had spent at the museum had pushed her to rediscover her love of research, her desire to write, and maybe even her passion for teaching. Over the course of the following autumn, she was hired by the American University in Paris, and it was now almost eight years that she had been lecturing in Renaissance art to American students who had been driven there by the most disparate of reasons, albeit in the majority of cases by romantic bents.

Unfortunately, she had realized, right from her first classes, that she would not be able to teach the way she had done in America. Given the lack of homogeneity in the students' level of English—but was it really a language problem or a form of intellectual decline?—she had been forced, over the years, to progressively simplify the critical readings by choosing easily legible ones with painstaking care. When in class, then, she had to make a supreme effort to entertain.

After so many years, there were still days in which she felt as if she were teaching a pack of deaf kids, as there was rarely a concept that did not need a supporting video, an image, or even—she was ashamed to say—some sort of comedic act. And yet, in spite of all this, for the first time in her life, she could claim that she was happy. The escape from Saranac Lake and afterward her New York stint had taught her that a small urban center was too narrow for her: she needed the anonymity of a big city, the necessary space to lose and find herself. Paris gave her access to a repertoire of archival works and materials she would have hardly found anywhere else, with the advantage that during moments of downtime, she could throw herself into forays through boutiques of perfumes, frills, flounces, and macarons. Every now and then, she found herself mulling over these projects, which had brought excitement to her departure. She had told herself that once in Paris, she would explore every inch of it, all the lesser-known corners. She wanted to trace a physical and mental map that would push her beyond herself, beyond her inveterate patterns and habits. But a year into the French capital and even this plan had been relegated to the bottom of a drawer, as often happens to good intentions when disconnected from concrete necessities. Tommaso, in the meantime, had grown. Mostly, he had gotten taller and at the same extraordinary speed of the small bean plant that day after day, he himself had watered untiringly. Having grown up in France, he nonetheless spoke to his mother in English.

But his version of it was a secondhand English, never fully mastered, never fully accepted, a bit like the woman allocated to him as a mother and who, more and more often, he treated as an intruder. By this time, almost an adolescent, he could consider himself French in every cadence, movement, and attitude of his: a quintessential Parisian, whose freedom of spirit had, more than once, thrown Leyla into an eddy of exhaustion. She regretted seeing him exclusively in increments of time, and when she came home in the evening after an afternoon he had spent with a friend or at a neighbor's, she discovered before her someone who had grown a couple of years. "What happened?" she asked herself, but it was one of those questions that had no answer, discharged as it was like a bullet that could only wound.

Deficient as a mother—at least according to her own standards—it didn't seem to Leyla as if she was having more success in caring for herself. She often had the impression that time was conspiring against her, that it was slithering out of her hands like a slippery bar of soap. In the meantime, her research responsibilities were accumulating nonstop and this due to the honor and glory of the French university system, which, while offering a renewed intellectual patina, obliged her to work at a rhythm that at her age weighed on her like forced labor. In the last few years, she had been invited to join a committee at the Louvre for the authentication of a *Judith and Holofernes* unearthed in Toulouse. Jacques, the head curator of the museum, was convinced that they were dealing with an original painting by Caravaggio, and red in the face, he frantically repeated the same four sentences to the journalists who consulted him for articles or radio interviews: "Look at the touch! Look at the skin tones! There is no doubt. It's the hand of the artist." To tell the truth, Jacques's insistence on the "magic hand" of the artist seemed vaguely onanistic to Leyla; yet one couldn't be too hard on him, especially when taking into account the short circuit between certainty and desire that not infrequently strikes middle-aged men. Of course, there were days she hoped that those last spurts of testosterone would be unleashed on thighs, hips, breasts . . . not on hers in any case. As for the rest, also due to her suspicion that the Toulouse canvas was a copy by a Flemish artist, her presence on the committee made her feel like the unfaithful bride in the hands of a religious fanatic.

Three Months Later

The Toulouse canvas told the story of Judith and Holofernes immortalized by artists of every era, well before Caravaggio devoted his talent to it. Now, the artist of the painting—whoever he was—had captured the moment in which the Jewish woman comes before the enemy's general, complete with a slave in tow, to seduce him, intoxicate him, and finally cut his head off. For the Louvre committee, the key element for attribution had been a copy of the picture, present in Neapolitan collections since time immemorial. And it was exactly the existence of this version *ab antiquo* that excited Jacques, convincing him of the authenticity of the Toulouse canvas and captivating him like a rekindled love. In fact, judging from the disjointed agitation he manifested at every meeting, Leyla intuited that the curator's sights should have been pouring over brawny male legs rather than on breasts and hips. In any case, she remained lukewarm. It seemed impossible to express a definitive judgment on the modes of exchange and imitation of the early seventeenth-century painters, but she was certain that Finson and Vinck had established a workshop in Naples specializing in copies of

Caravaggio. The Toulouse canvas might have been one of their many specimens. In fact, to the best of her recollection, Caravaggio was short of money at this time, and so the fact that he had contacted this gang of forgers—whether for reasons of interest or immediate necessity—wasn't something to dismiss.

However, it was particularly difficult to distinguish the copies from the originals, just as it was impossible to recognize the many hands that teamed up at various times to work on these canvases. Gina, a Sicilian colleague of hers, often whispered disdainfully, "Can you imagine if we, foreign scholars that we are, were able to convince the head curator of the Louvre to abandon the discovery of the century? These are the French. They're always right. You know, right like mules." And so it was that even this assignment at the Louvre—as Leyla grumbled when she was alone—had been transformed into a titanic effort, a futile enterprise destined to leave her empty-handed, like everything in her life, including, in this strangely gloomy August, her onerous motherhood, which she had so strenuously wanted, tenaciously protected but which was already reduced to a feeble trickle and, like that trickle, destined to be submerged by the quicksand of time.

It was already weeks since she had been spending at least half of her day in interminable and inconclusive meetings. The secret of the *Judith* was still impenetrable and—as her French colleagues, with the exception of Jacques, were beginning to recognize—would presumably remain so. Then one day, she caught sight of him in the museum. A shadowy figure sneaked up on her. It was the ghost of Michael, an apparition that unlike this painting would soon become a riddle with a solution. Yet, when she came home, she began to doubt herself. She wondered if Michael's appearance was nothing more than an image generated by her perpetual state of somnolence, a look-alike, a trick of the imagination, like the profile of Pablo, which in the last few weeks had surreptitiously crawled over Tommaso's face. She struggled to believe that it was almost eight years since the news of Pablo's death had reached her via a long and roundabout pathway. In fact, friends from Saranac Lake with whom she had stayed in contact despite the distance had found a considerate but somewhat maudlin way to apprise her of this incident: "He was the father of her son and he died," they had stammered repeatedly. "Maybe they shouldn't get mixed up in it, but they felt an obligation to do so." During those telephone conversations, Leyla had felt a chest spasm that at the time seemed superficial; "It will heal," she had told herself. Unfortunately, the ache remained inside, becoming ingrained, and the infection spread slowly but irrevocably. Since her breakup with Pablo, she had often repeated to herself that if one day Tommaso were to ask her if he could meet his father, she would not do anything to prevent it. On the contrary, she kept rehearsing a mental script in which at Tommaso's timid and circumspect questions, she would urge him to seek out his father, reassuring him that she would not be the least bit upset. The sudden and "frankly ill-mannered" death of Pablo, however, had catapulted her into the role of ungenerous mother, burrower into a past world, responsible for the dearth of feelings that followed his sudden disappearance. Real or imaginary as it might have been, Michael's presence in Paris gave her hope that a possible channel toward that little old world, however insubstantial, still existed. Assuming that it had actually been Michael that she had seen—a thought that made her shudder—and assuming that the ghosts of long ago hadn't swept away her already shaky sense of reality as well. Then again, she wondered in despair, "Is it really possible to find a needle in a haystack?"

She had to focus, think schematically. She had told herself that those same friends who had informed her of Pablo's death had to possess some additional knowledge about Michael. After months of thinking what kind of message to send, she wrote them a short email. An answer arrived after a few minutes as if they had been waiting for months, glued to the screen. They revealed to her that following her departure from Saranac Lake, Michael and Pablo got together again. They had met up in southern Italy to which, as far as they knew, Michael had run off after he had finished his studies. Unfortunately, if in the first weeks of his Neapolitan sojourn, Pablo had sent a few hurried messages, after a few months, communication had come to an abrupt end. "We're sorry," they cut it short, "but we have no idea where he might be now, and we don't think anyone here in Saranac Lake knows much more than we do." In their email, however, they took it for granted that he might still be in Naples, but they couldn't exclude the possibility that he had not moved elsewhere. In short, they couldn't confirm or deny what Leyla had thought she had seen in Paris. The email ended with points of ellipsis, almost as if Leyla could replace Pablo as their pen pal, but these were ravings caused by loneliness, she brooded. Her only hope, then, was that of bumping into Michael or his look-alike at the Louvre. The odds of this happening were in the realm of the absurd, one of those off-the-chart numbers that so fascinated her as a young girl in math class. She understood that if the man glimpsed at the Louvre turned out to be Michael, the most probable option was that he was there in transit like a hundred other day tourists; but if she had learned one thing about Michael—considering how little she had associated

with him at Saint Luke and therefore relying on the salacious stories of her more gossipy female students—she had
learned that there was no initiative to which he might be
attracted by pure chance or, on a whim, no action that he
would take spontaneously. All in all, if Michael had come to
the Louvre, there had to be a reason and that reason could
make him come back.

The meetings of the committee for the attribution to
Caravaggio of the *Judith and Holofernes* became more and
more frequent, and yet, perhaps due to skepticism or to a new
resolution, the breaks that Leyla allowed herself also inten-
sified. She would get up and leave to her colleagues' dismay,
darting out from the room as if in sudden need of a toilet.
But in her view, she was leaving behind inconclusive discussions to seek out her fate. So at each and every failure, at
every mad dash around the Louvre, she grew stronger in the
conviction that her encounter with Michael was imminent,
that her leaps into the void were about to bring them closer.
It was the ticktock of a clock. And she was right. On the first
of June, they stood in front of each other, shadows under
their eyes and spotlights above them, their gazes fixed on
each other, and behind them, the lifeless body of the *Death
of the Virgin* by Caravaggio.

They took each other by the hand and walked for about thirty
minutes without exchanging a word. They roamed the corridors of the Louvre thrusting their feet one ahead of the
other in a daze, like the blind on a ship at the mercy of a
storm. "I'm really happy to see you. I was afraid that my eyes
were playing tricks on me. I'm sorry. . . . I'm not explaining
myself well. . . . What I wanted to say is that . . ." Michael
interrupted her: "Never mind! Really! Why don't we find a

place where we can have a coffee? Let's get out of here."
Plunged into silence after Michael's directive, they marched
triumphantly along the Rue du Louvre as if they were parting
the waters of the Red Sea, as if the entire city was observing them from afar. They then turned into the Rue Étienne
Marcel and a bit by chance arrived at the Café Montorgueil.
A quick exchange of glances and they understood this was
the place. Leyla asked the waiter for a table close to the sidewalk, then, having obtained a nod of assent, she slid down
onto a wrought-iron chair. They both did. From where they
were seated, they could see Stohrer's pastry shop, with
its flashy yellow-and-blue awning. Turning toward her,
Michael exclaimed, "Do you know that Stohrer's is where
Naples's most famous desserts were invented? All because
of an unhappy queen. Her name escapes me now . . . the
baba, for example." Leyla stared at him with a look in her
eyes begging him to stop. For both of them, like for those
queens of old, it had been about comings and goings, eva-
sions and escapes at the edge of an abyss. All of a sudden,
she burst into tears, all the while wondering why the word
"baba" had triggered such a discordant reaction, so out of
place, so tragicomical. "Forgive me. It's not your fault," she
said. "It's the fault of the too-many moves. It's the fault of
my son. I must have wanted him too much. I had him too
late." Then, noticing that Michael was examining her, perplexed and distant, as if on a different planet, she abruptly
steered the conversation toward its would-be nerve center.
"Do you miss Pablo?" she asked. Without needing to say it,
they had made Pablo the currency of their exchange, and
seated like thieves in this Parisian café, they wished to offer
him the service he never had at his death. "Tell me, where
are you living here in Paris? Tell me about Tommaso. Tell
me everything!" he commanded her, ignoring her question

with an archaic smile. And that was how in the hours that followed, they leafed through their lives in review, Leyla telling him of her multiple displacements and relocations, of the Louvre committee and obviously about Jacques with his thousand twitches and twinges; Michael revealing to Leyla, and perhaps to himself for the first time, that it was time to find a new place. About Pablo, however, they said very little, almost nothing. Michael gave her the details she did not have. He told her of the body, of how he had been found dead in a dumpster. She bowed her head and winced in pain. They recognized that they were both living existences of an abnormal loneliness. Michael had had bed companions, rarely a lover. Leyla, instead, had been single for years and only recently had been dating a colleague, not without some wariness and constant hesitancies on both sides. It was a relationship of convenience, she concluded, made easier by his ex-wife, children, the thousand responsibilities by which the man was still constrained. Michael and Leyla had no need to make promises when, after about two hours, they left each other and went back to their respective routines. But from this first meeting and in the coming weeks, not a day would go by in which Leyla and Michael didn't see each other, exchange a telephone call, or again intertwine the threads of their unresolved lives.

EPILOGUE

~ 13 ~

Michael

If, in the Saranac Lake period of his life, a psychic had shown him the path that he would take, Michael would have greeted the prediction with an unequivocal laugh, convinced that the future could not be written on the palm of a hand. Now, however—quite amusingly—he regretted that he had not met that palm reader. Perhaps he would have been more vigilant, more ready to fight that part of his own destiny that had begun within him. From the time that Leyla and Tommaso entered his life, it seemed as if he were starting over. He played the role of uncle, hoping to be treated as a father. He knew that for many years Tommaso had been starved of this type of interaction. For his part, Tommaso asked Michael questions that he had never asked of Leyla, secretly wishing to borrow memories of Pablo that she would not have known how to offer. Events moved forward at a hectic pace. Over the course of the previous summer, Leyla and Michael had both decided to move to the fourteenth arrondissement: Leyla, with Tommaso, on the Avenue du Maine, he himself on the Rue d'Alésia. Their houses were five minutes apart, and Michael covered that stretch of road like a shuttle, punctually showing up at dinnertime with some prepared treat. Without having to say it, they had decided to create a family bubble. From time to time, Michael and Tommaso left the Marais district to say hello to Merwan, who had taken to absenting himself more and more often to give some space to his daughter. But except for the baker, Michael didn't miss anything from his old neighborhood, which meant that he didn't miss the sporadic sexual encounters, the seasonal boyfriends, the always cheerful crowds of tourists. He was beginning to wonder at what moment along this righteous journey of his he had taken a wrong turn. . . .

~ 14 ~

Leyla

They say that the fruit doesn't fall far from the tree, and already for a while now, Leyla had begun to realize what Tommaso's preferences and interests were. The classmates with whom he got along best were Brune and Carla, the best looking in the class, the most mature, and the most impertinent. And then there was Amid. Amid played soccer, looked at older girls, and had all the passion and disdain of a typical teenager. Tommaso, on the other hand, only had eyes for Amid, his soccer player legs, his hands; the problem was that with only the language of an adolescent at his disposal, he couldn't find the right words to describe his feelings. This is why the constant presence of Michael lifted a weight off Leyla's chest. Finally, Tommaso had a man to guide him where she could not. As in an upside-down *Divine Comedy*, then, Virgil followed Beatrice, the man followed the woman, and instead of an ascent to the heavens, the journey appeared to be a retreat to the underworld. Her true hope? That Tommaso might not suffer too much.

"Are you sure that you don't mind being alone on New Year's? What are you thinking of doing? We can always change our flight and leave a few days later." Eyeing her up and down like a stray dog, Tommaso repeated his slippery questions and appeals, albeit knowing, or at least hoping, that his mother would not change her mind. In fact, for over a month now, he and Michael had been planning their Christmas trip to the United States, seated around the kitchen table like generals on the eve of battle. Out of politeness, she answered, "Don't worry, Tommaso. Your mother is old. She doesn't wish anything other than twelve hours of uninterrupted sleep for New Year's," but she would have liked to add, "Enough with this pretense of concern, these theatrics. Let's change the subject." Indeed, of the three of them, she was the only one to realize that this trip to the United States was the only subject about which they had talked since that rather fateful evening at the end of November, when Michael had received "the call"; since that evening in November that is, when he had been informed that his mother was in hospital, practically on the brink of death. Among other things, Leyla didn't know how to hide her annoyance at the fact that a courtesy visit to a woman on her dying bed had become for Michael and her son a pretext for a trip that sooner or later they would have taken anyway. In fact, they were counting on going back to Manhattan after the visit to the Saranac Lake Hospital. From there, they would leave for a coast-to-coast journey, passing through Chicago, and finishing their tour in San Francisco. She wondered if, in her role of mother, she was supposed to prohibit, forbid, or temper her son's enthusiasm. She thought back to the spell that

Pablo had whispered into Tommaso's ear the day of their separation, around thirteen years earlier. She feared that it might now be brought to fruition. Although stubbornly denying it to herself, Leyla had already known that her devoted son would one day become an enemy. It was a few days before their departure, and tired of the fact that Tommaso was always taking Michael's side, one evening she yelled at him, "All right, Michael is always right, but this *you love me, you love me not* game is beginning to grow tiresome." "You're really an idiot," Tommaso sarcastically fired back. "In the first place, comparing yourself to a wilted flower doesn't do you justice. Then again, worst-case scenario, you can always join us in New York." He hurt her, therefore, with the cruelty natural to adolescence, but he did it because in a recently revealed corner of his consciousness, he felt that it had been his mother who had neglected him and not the other way around. As a matter of fact, since Michael had taken over the role of father, Leyla had begun to withdraw, even if gradually and with no plan in mind. It was Michael who went to pick up Tommaso on the evenings he stayed over at his friends'. It was he who cooked for everyone. It was he who always sat through those interminable fencing competitions, and it was he who corrected Tommaso's essays, who always rewrote them hastily. Leyla could not remember her last parent-teacher conference, the last time that her presence had been requested either in the family or in school. In the last few weeks, Michael and Tommaso had taken up the habit of lunching together while she was at work, and after lunch—when she came home to prep her courses and do her correcting—they would always disappear with the excuse of a new pastime, an umpteenth, not-to-be-missed event: a film to see at the movie theater, an exhibit, a game of bocce with the elderly pensioners of the neighborhood.

Of this bizarre family she was the least surprised when from bocce they graduated to playful wrestling, from that to physically clinging to each other, to lengthier and closer contacts. She told herself they were the hugs of a father, but she couldn't help but notice them, to not be unnerved by this behavior. This departure for the United States therefore exonerated her of all responsibility. She felt free for the first time in years.

She was secretly observing Tommaso, almost as if the boy were a kitten who had escaped the litter, a pet to let wander around the house. Tommaso was torturing Michael: "What do you think I should wear in America? What's the weather like in Saranac Lake? I imagine I need a heavy jacket, but I don't have anything like that. Maybe a ski jacket would work or an army jacket . . . like what you used in Vietnam during the war." He came out with similar absurdities to check whether Michael was listening to him, and he would get annoyed when he saw Michael nodding without moving his eyelids, occasionally turning toward Leyla in search of an ally. In fact, from the moment they had decided to spend Christmas in America, Michael was living in a parallel dimension. The idea of seeing his mother again after so many years had reopened an abyss of anxieties, feelings of guilt, and profound sadness in him. He felt as if he were being pulled down, and it was clear that he sought in Tommaso a buoy that might keep him afloat. Tommaso, on the other hand, felt that Michael seemed absent and distracted. He was incapable of sympathizing with him. Rather, he tried to understand what might be his role on this trip: was he supposed to play the role of son, nephew, something else? "I can look for one of my old winter coats," Michael yelled to him from the room, as if to tell him that he was still there and that he had noticed his diva-like exit. And then he added,

"I think that a Vietnamese military jacket might be too light for thirty below. Stop worrying. I'm listening to you." He wanted to make sure Tommaso understood that not a single sentence of his was lost on him, that all his gestures and intentions would get through any kind of drowsiness he might be exhibiting, in other words that Tommaso was "heard." And at his "I'm listening to you," Leyla was also startled. While that verb "listening" rolled between her mind and her throat like a caged hamster, she found herself wondering if there were a single person in the whole world who had actually ever listened . . . to her. She glanced over at the book *Atheism Conquered* by Campanella. After many years, Michael had returned it to her. She had lent him the book when he was her student. Gazing at this historical relic, Leyla recalled the long and winding journey of this Calabrian Dominican and how no one had listened to his theories because they were ahead of their time when he first shared them and because they eventually turned him into a curious animal as he proclaimed them to the bitter end at the court of Louis XIV. As had happened to them, Campanella had begun a new life in Paris, but "alas," ruminated Leyla with melancholy, there existed second chances that come too late. Now there were only a few days left before their departure. Tommaso covered up the silences and the embarrassment, dramatically exaggerating the possible difficulties of the trip, lamenting his lack of clothes and accoutrements that, once in the United States, he thought would be practically impossible to resolve. Michael, on the other hand, counted on packing whatever was necessary at the very last minute. The thought of the upcoming meeting with his mother was overwhelming to him. He didn't know whether he had more fear of finding his mother already dead or of having to subject her to the rigmarole of awkward and banal excuses.

He felt that everything would be even more painful in a hospital room and that he would not have the courage to raise his voice had his mother lost some of her hearing. Tommaso quietly reentered the room. He tenderly hugged Michael and said, "Don't be afraid! She's still your mother. Mothers forgive everything, don't they, Leyla?" A liberating laugh escaped her. When all was said and done, this boy, who called her by her name, who comforted everyone with the peremptory wisdom of the elderly had been a gift from above. How much normality, how much pointless scandal would reign over their ragtag lives? Contrary to Caravaggio's heroines, then, she would not persist in begging for the love of sons, fathers, or transitory men. She took a look at the weather forecast for the entire month of December: Michael and Tommaso would arrive in America in time for the first snowfall. As for her, all she had to do was get ready for the sweetest, most unjustified, and solitary of confinements.

Notes on Contributors

ALESSANDRO GIARDINO is chair and associate professor of Italian and French literature at Saint Lawrence University in Canton, New York. Born in Naples in 1985, he studied at the University of Bologna, the University of California, Berkeley, and McGill University, specializing in modern and contemporary art history, as well as Mediterranean minorities literature. Giardino has published two academic books and written articles on Giorgio Bassani, Françoise Sagan, Marguerite Yourcenar, and more recently, Leïla Slimani for numerous international journals. For the last ten years, Giardino has been part of a research group on the Neapolitan baroque movement. In 2020, his bilingual newsletter *X-Ray: Il corpo di Napoli / The Body of Naples* has brought together hundreds of readers on both sides of the Atlantic.

JOYCE MYERSON is a professional academic and literary translator from Italian. Her translations of books on medieval history as well as art and architecture (*Stories of Women in the Middle Ages* by Maria Teresa Brolis, *A Life of Ill Repute, Public Prostitution in the Middle Ages* by Maria Serena Mazzi, *The Cistercian Arts*, and *The Evolving European City*) have all been published within the last ten years. Her translation of a book of two *canzoni* by the fourteenth century Tuscan poet,

Andrea Pucci, was published in 2013. More recently she has been translating articles for professional journals dealing with psychoanalysis and psychotherapy. Her translation of the book *History of Countertransference: From Freud to the British Object Relations School* by Alberto Stefana was published in 2017. Her translation of the book, *Psychopathology of the Situation in Gestalt Therapy*, edited by Margherita Spagnuolo Lobb and Pietro Andrea Cavaleri was published in 2023.

ARA H. MERJIAN is professor of Italian studies at New York University, where he is an affiliate of the Institute of Fine Arts and the Department of Art History. He is a member of the College of Professors in the Department of History, University of Milan, and the author of *Giorgio de Chirico and the Metaphysical City: Nietzsche, Modernism, Paris* and *Against the Avant-Garde: Pier Paolo Pasolini, Contemporary Art, and Neocapitalism.*